JACK FLINT
AND THE
DARK WAYS

Also by Joe Donnelly

Jack Flint and the Redthorn Sword
Jack Flint and the Spellbinder's Curse

JACK FLINT AND THE DARK WAYS

JOE DONNELLY

Illustrated by Geoff Taylor

Orion
Children's Books

First published in Great Britain in 2010
by Orion Children's Books
a division of the Orion Publishing Group Ltd
Orion House
5 Upper St Martin's Lane
London WC2H 9EA
An Hachette UK Company

1 3 5 7 9 10 8 6 4 2

A catalogue record for this book
is available from the British Library

ISBN 978 1 84255 583 5

Typeset by Input Data Services Ltd,
Bridgwater, Somerset

Printed in Great Britain by Clays Ltd, St Ives plc

www.orionbooks.co.uk

To George McKechnie,

who always knew a good story

WHAT HAS GONE BEFORE

Jack Flint had never felt so completely alone in his life.

It was time to make a hard decision. He knew that.

Since the day he and Kerry Malone stumbled through the ring of standing stones in Cromwath Blackwood they had faced real danger time and time again.

When they stepped between the ancient stones, they found themselves on a bloodied battlefield in the legendary world of Temair. There, they had befriended the chieftain's daughter, Corriwen Redthorn, and fought their way together across the country, harried by Scree ogres and by the mad Mandrake's henchmen, guided by the ancient Book of Ways *and somehow protected by the heartstone key which opened the gates to the lands of myth.*

It was in Temair that Jack first found clues to the identity of the father he had never met; the first bearer of the mysterious heartstone that Jack now wore around his neck. He gradually realised that his father had been a traveller between the worlds, a hero who fought on the side of good. A Journeyman.

Then Jack, Kerry and Corriwen had faced the devastating power behind Mandrake's reign of evil: the monstrous spirit of destruction known as the Morrigan.

In the final confrontation they had barely escaped with their lives, but in the battle with the Morrigan, Corriwen was thrown through another mystical gate and vanished into a different world. Jack and Kerry set out to rescue her, and found themselves in Eirinn, a world Jack knew only from the legends he had read in old books.

And Eirinn was no less perilous than Temair. Dermott the Wolf and his dark spellbinder Fainn hunted them from one side of the land to the other in pursuit of the Harp of Tara.

It was not until they met Hedda the Scatha, the ferocious warrior woman, that Jack, Kerry and Corriwen and Connor, the rightful King of Eirinn, stopped running and began to fight back. Hedda had befriended Jack's father, the Journeyman Hero whose task was to protect the mythic worlds. She gave Jack a new-forged sword, identical to the one his father had wielded and Jack knew then that his own quest would be to find him, no matter what dangers he might face.

With the help of friends they had made in the fight against Dermott and Fainn, they faced their enemies near the magical Tara Hill where the harp's song summoned the Sky Queen, the ancient goddess of peace and harmony.

There, Jack was given yet another clue about his long-lost father.

Now, back in the ring of standing stones, his mind was made up. It was no easy decision.

Whatever the cost, Jack would venture once again through the mythic gates, and this time he would travel alone.

ONE

Blinding flashes seared Jack's eyes and he experienced the familiar sensation of being turned completely inside out, with every nerve pulled thin like a spiderweb, every cell split and scattered. Colours raced past him as if he was falling down a well that went on forever. Cold shuddered through him like spears of ice.

Then there was a twisting sensation and he was on his knees, hauling for breath and gagging against the nausea that bubbled up from deep inside.

It took him a moment to realise he was kneeling in the sunshine and the air was warm and clean.

The door into summer.

Behind him, the standing stones stood out against a deep blue sky, each smooth and polished, carved with strange figures and stranger script, but Jack knew each figure and each word was part of the power that let the gates open and close. Between them, the air twisted and warped, spangling with strange luminescence. Beyond the stones, grass swayed in the light breeze. Somewhere high above, a lark soared.

Still gripping the long sword tight, the gift from Hedda the warrior woman, Jack raised himself to his feet and looked around. Pollen scented the air. In the distance, rolling hills faded in summer haze. A perfect day in any world.

Yet Jack Flint thought he had never felt so completely alone in his life.

He let out a slow breath.

'Well,' he said to himself. 'That's it now. I'm here.'

Wherever *here* was.

Jack took a tentative step forward, then another, until he reached a stream. There, he knelt down, cupped a hand and took a sip. The water was cold and refreshing. He dabbed at his eyes, wiping away tears that had come unbidden and refused to be blinked back.

Ahead of him, somewhere in this world, was something that would lead him to his goal. It was here, he now believed, that he would find the route to his past. The route to the father he had never known.

This was not Corriwen's quest, nor Kerry's, though Corriwen's only brother lay dead at Mandrake's hands on the slaughterfield in Temair. Though Kerry's father was cooling his heels in Drumbain Jail back home after his failed poaching attempt almost destroyed the old bridge. They had their own destinies to seek, and he would not lead them into more danger.

Jack's father, Jonathan Cullian Flint might be alive and he might be dead, but his son had to know for sure, had to discover the truth.

He stood again, ready to take the first steps on his journey in this new world.

But before he could take a step, the air was rent apart by a sudden screech. In a second it rose to a crescendo, like a jet racing up a runway. Then something struck him with such force he stumbled back, twisting to grab his sword.

'Wha . . .?'

Something else hit him and sent him tumbling to land on his backside.

The screeching stopped abruptly. A hollow *pop* sucked out what breath he had left in his lungs. He struggled against the weight and something struggled against *him*.

'Jeez, Jack,' Kerry Malone bawled in his ear. 'I'm just *never* going to get used to going through those gates.'

A small hand grabbed his own and heaved him to his feet as his vision cleared.

'Are you all right?' Corriwen sounded concerned.

She spoke softly in his ear. Jack shook his head to steady himself. Corriwen and Kerry faced him on the grass. And beyond the two stones, the spangling lights were gone. All he could see were hills rolling away in the distance. The gate was closed.

'What are you two doing here?' Joy and dismay wrestled inside him.

'Aw, Jack,' Kerry said. 'What else could we do? You know

you'll just get into a mess if we're not here to watch your back.'

'One for all,' Corriwen said earnestly. 'Isn't that what you said?'

'And each for everybody else,' Kerry interjected. 'Like always.'

'You were supposed to go home!'

'Yeah, right. And let you have all the fun?'

Even Corriwen laughed. 'We talked,' she said. 'Temair will still be Temair without me for a while.'

'And there's not much for me back home,' Kerry added. 'I'm a nobody there. Here I'm ... hell, I don't even know where this is.'

He looked around him, smelling the nectar on the air, feeling the sun on his face.

'But it sure is a whole lot better than the other places you took me to. No bodies, no monsters. And it's *warm*!'

He knuckled Jack on the shoulder. 'It's like being on holiday, and we're due a break, don't you think? This place looks just great.'

Jack was speechless. He felt tears prick in his eyes again and this time he just managed to blink them away. Without a word he dropped the sword, swung his arms around his friends and hugged them tight.

'Oh, quit that,' Kerry protested. 'You'll have me blubberin' for sure.'

It was sometime in the afternoon, Kerry guessed from where the sun sat low in the sky, and they hadn't wandered far from the two standing stones.

'I love this place,' Kerry said. He'd taken Corriwen down to the stream and shown her how to catch fish, poacher-style, with his bare hands, tickling them out from under the banks and flat stones.

'They swim right into your hands,' he said, between mouthfuls of freshly cooked fish that might have been trout but were as pink inside as salmon. The brushwood fire glowed and gave off the scent of herbs. Above it, in the aromatic smoke, three more fat fish were cooking slowly to a rich brown. 'This is paradise, I swear.'

Corriwen had collected herbs and nuts from a grove on the hillside, and black damsons as big as apples from the shrubs alongside the stream. She sighed and leant back against a smooth river-stone.

'It *is* peaceful,' she said. Jack had to agree, but under his thought came another: Yes, but will it stay that way?

As if sensing his doubt, Corriwen glanced at him curiously.

'I think we should try to find out where we are,' Jack said.

'Yeah,' Kerry chuckled. 'Get out the old sat-nav!'

Corriwen gave him one of her puzzled looks and both boys laughed.

'You'd never believe me if I told you what that was,' Kerry said.

Jack had been putting off the moment, content to be with Corriwen and Kerry. Today had felt like a picnic and

Kerry was right, they'd needed a break. But now he reached into his satchel and drew out the old book, feeling its weight in his hands.

The ancient leather binding was as familiar to him now as all the books on the shelf beside his bed back home, though none was as mysterious or as important.

The *Book of Ways* twisted in his palm, as if it contained a life of its own. The front cover flipped open to let the leaves whirr of their own volition until they stopped at a blank page.

Kerry and Corriwen crowded close, watching intently as old script gradually appeared on the page, line by line. Jack looked at Kerry. 'You read it, if you like.'

When the words stopped etching themselves Kerry began to speak.

The Farward Gate of Vaine dear
The Summerland so Fair and Clear
But Journeyman should well step light
For mischief stalks the bleak of night.
Spell miscast for binder's gain
Summons shadow, summons bane.

Set face and foot to Westward path
And shelter fast from bale-moon wrath
Journeyman must face his fate
For nowhere now stands homeward gate
In darkness deep waits darkness old
And peril waits who seeks his goal.

Kerry stopped, and for a moment there was silence.

'Not very promising,' Jack finally said.

'It never is,' Kerry responded. 'I wish just once it would tell us straight. And maybe it's got it wrong. This place seems okay to me.'

'And Temair was once your oh-kay too,' Corriwen interrupted. 'But where there's good, there is always bad.'

'Maybe not as bad as before,' Jack said, though his mind kept repeating the words from the second verse: *Nowhere now stands homeward gate.*

He felt those fingers of uncertainty creep on the skin of his back. He had come on a quest, hoping he had chosen the right gate. If he was wrong, if there was no way back . . .

Jack shook the thought away and closed the book.

'I think the holiday is over,' he said.

TWO

The sun hovered on the horizon before it finally sank from view. A bright flicker of green was followed by a wave of strange purple light which rolled across the sky.

'Weird,' Kerry said.

'That sometimes happens,' Jack said. 'The green flash at sunset. I read it somewhere.'

'Not that.' Kerry was looking towards where the sun had set. He pointed. Jack and Corriwen stood beside him.

Behind them, the sky was silken black and dotted with stars and a full moon glowed silver. But in the distance ahead, a bruised haze swelled on the horizon, swirling like oil on a stagnant pool.

'Is that a storm coming on? Everywhere we go, there's always a freakin' storm. You'd think we could get a break!'

'I don't like this,' Corriwen whispered, almost to herself.

Jack nodded. He looked around them as a breeze began to rise, bringing with it a faint whiff of burning.

'We're a bit exposed here,' he said.

Kerry drew his eyes away from the strange haze. 'I saw some trees over the hill,' he said. 'Maybe we should shelter there for the night.'

The line in the *Book of Ways* echoed in Jack's mind: *For mischief stalks the bleak of night.*

'Sooner the better,' Corriwen said, and packed the remaining food into their bags. Jack stashed the book and gathered his sword and the amberhorn bow while Kerry wrapped the smoked fish in big leaves then trotted down to a pool in the stream and hacked out an armful of tall bulrushes.

'Torches,' he explained to no one in particular. 'They burn.'

'Good thinking,' Jack said. Kerry was always practical. They made their way quickly up the slope to the coppice which covered the crest, while the purple haze expanded like a dark squall towards them. They were only a few yards from the shelter of the overhanging boughs when Kerry stopped abruptly.

'What is it?' Corriwen said, peering ahead into the shadows. From the corner of his eye, Jack caught a silver flicker and knew that she had drawn her knives.

'Not there,' Kerry said. He pointed over her head and the three of them looked up at the sky.

The dark tinge was beginning to brush past the full moon, casting shadows over its face. As it thickened, the silver faded to violet. For a long moment the moon was completely obscured, and then it waxed bright again.

Now it glared down at them, red as blood, its surface seeming to writhe.

'Jeez, Jack,' Kerry breathed. 'It's just like ...'

'The night we saw Billy Robbins,' Jack finished for him. The night – it seemed so long ago now – that Billy Robbins had hunted them through the trees behind the Major's home, the moon had turned blood-red. And with it had come an awful darkness that had oozed its way into the Major's study and caused their fearful flight through the tunnel into Cromwath Blackwood and on through the gates to another world.

Under that red moon, the Nightshades had ripped into their own world and come hunting. Jack knew now that they were searching for the mystical heartstone he wore.

'Nightshades,' Kerry whispered. 'Do you think they're from here?'

Cold prickles made the hair on Jack's neck stand on end. Below his collarbone, the heartstone shuddered, sending him a warning.

Corriwen made a quick gesture with her fingers. Jack didn't know what it meant, but he could guess. She was warding off something bad.

'Come on,' he said, gripping her by the elbow. 'Let's get into cover.'

He turned one last time. Behind him, the Farward Gate reflected the blood-light, two red pillars.

Ahead of them, Kerry stumbled. Jack heard the crack of dry wood snapping.

'What's up?'

'Some kind of fence,' Kerry said. 'I tripped over it.'

Corriwen helped Kerry to his feet. Two halves of a thin branch hung from a pair of slender uprights. It was part of a frail barrier, though what it could have corralled Jack couldn't imagine. Small corn-dolls, woven from golden straw, hung from the horizontal struts, dancing in the odd light.

'Stupid place to put a fence,' Kerry said, stepping gingerly towards the trees. Under the first leafy boughs, they were out of the direct glare of the red moon and Jack felt less nervous. They moved on until they found a small dell. Kerry collected some twigs and pulled out the little lighter that had already served them well in two worlds. He bent over the pile, flicked the lighter and jerked back as a six-inch flame almost singed his eyebrows.

'Nearly blinded myself there,' he said, rubbing his eye. 'The adjuster must be jammed.'

He managed to start the fire and used the flames to ignite the bulrush heads before jamming the stalks into the ground to give them more light.

They sat close together in silence, each with their own thoughts, each peering now and again into the gloom beyond the glow of the torches.

'What do you think the book was trying to say?' Kerry's question broke the silence.

Jack closed his eyes, recalling each word, the way he'd remembered lines of poetry in school.

'It says this place is Uaine.'

'Ooh-waine?'

'That's how you say it. I remember it from the legends

in the Major's books, like Temair and Eirinn. It's old, anyway. It was a magical place.'

'It seemed like that when we first came,' Corriwen said. She shivered. The breeze, even in the trees, was colder now despite the heat from the fire. 'Now it doesn't feel right.'

'Mischief stalks the bleak of night,' Jack recited. He could feel the heartstone pulse slowly on his chest. 'And shelter fast from bale moon wrath.'

'Doesn't sound like a lot of fun and games,' Kerry said.

'No,' Jack said flatly. 'But it got the moon right, so we have to be on guard tonight.'

'You bet,' Kerry said. 'I don't think I could sleep anyway.'

But in half an hour, Kerry was curled up close to the embers, head on his backpack, snoring softly. Jack and Corriwen faced each other beside the fire. Jack noticed the flickering flames made her hair gleam. She reached into her bag, pulled out some of the big nuts, and threw one to Jack.

'You bear the key to all worlds. That's what the Sky Lady said.'

Jack nodded. 'I think I knew that already. She called me a Journeyman. That's what my father was. But she couldn't tell me where he had gone. I've got to find that out for myself.' *Now your own quest begins,* the lady had told him.

'She said to find the door into summer. And then the door into night. Whatever that means,' he said, remembering.

Jack ignored the goosebumps rising on his skin and smiled at Corriwen. 'But we'll find out soon enough.' He stretched out a hand and took hers. 'At least I'm not alone.'

'No, Jack. We wouldn't let that happen.' She smiled back at him. 'One for all.'

He was about to respond with Kerry's usual reply when a sudden cry startled both of them.

Kerry rolled and was on his knees in an instant, eyes wide and bewildered.

'Bad dream?' Jack asked.

Kerry nodded, short of breath. He rubbed his eyes with shaky hands.

'Just like when I was little. I used to dream there were things under the bed, crawling out to get me. It scared me to death.'

'But you're not in your bed,' Jack said.

'Something hit me,' Kerry said. 'Was it you?'

'Don't be daft,' Jack said, but as he spoke, he heard a soft thumping sound. Kerry jerked backwards.

'Did you see that?' He pointed at his backpack. The thud came again and the backpack bucked of its own accord.

'A bristlehog,' Corriwen said. 'It must have crawled in.' She giggled. 'Just don't eat it. They're foul, and I should know. It was sometimes all I had to eat when Mandrake's ogres hunted me.'

Kerry drew his short-sword and eased it under the flap, flicked the blade and the bag opened flat. Something moved inside and he bent closer to warily peer in.

One of the trout he'd cooked earlier flopped out and quivered on the ground. Its tail flipped up, once, twice. Kerry really jerked back this time.

'This isn't happening!' He rapped his head with a

knuckle, realised he wasn't dreaming and looked, pale-faced at the others. 'It's dead. How can it be . . .?'

Corriwen squawked and her hand opened. The nut dropped, rolled between the stones around the fire and for a second everybody's attention was away from the impossibly flopping fish. The nutshell cracked open and a pair of black legs poked through, as a big black spider scraped its way out. Its legs pawed the air and two glittering fangs raised up, little drips of poison forming at their tips. It moved in a blur of legs and ran up Corriwen's ankle, red eyes glittering.

Without a pause Kerry swung his blade and flicked the spider off into the fire where it stumbled around sizzling until it crumpled into a smoking ball.

'Something's wrong here,' Kerry said shakily. The dead trout flipped again, its mouth opening and snapping shut. Two rows of jagged piranha-like teeth gnashed together with every snap; teeth that had not been there when Kerry hauled it from the stream.

The fish convulsed again, landing near Kerry's foot. The teeth would have taken a chunk out of him if he hadn't kicked it away fast. Corriwen snatched up a stone and clobbered it flat before it could move again.

Way beyond the firelight, in the deep gloom of the trees, a low moan, like an animal in pain, came through the darkness, breaking into stuttering gasps as it echoed from tree to tree.

Mischief stalks the bleak of night. The *Book of Ways* had got that right, Jack thought.

He got to his feet and then Corriwen was at his side.

Kerry joined them and they stood back to back, shoulder to shoulder, weapons ready.

'This is as bad as being in the open,' Kerry whispered. Beyond the firelight, the low moan shivered again through the forest and under that, even deeper still, came the hungry grunting sound of some beast on the hunt.

One of the bulrush torches guttered and sent a trail of smoke twirling up. It writhed and then condensed slowly until they could make out what seemed to be a gargoyle face. A long tendril oozed out and slowly formed a thin hand which snatched at Corriwen's neck. Jack pulled her back before it could touch her. The ghastly face stretched into an evil grin before the breeze wafted it away.

'Was that real?' Corriwen asked, shuddering.

'I don't know,' Jack whispered.

'That freakin' fish was real,' Kerry said. 'Nearly had my foot off. It was like a shark.'

In the shadows, Jack thought he could detect movement and the heartstone began to quiver. Kerry felt him tense.

'I really don't think we should stay here,' he whispered.

'It might be worse out there,' Corriwen said.

'No,' Jack said clearly. 'I can see things in the shadows. I don't know what they are, but I've got a bad feeling.' His sword was drawn, the Scatha's blade, razor-sharp and deadly, but somehow he thought even this sword might be useless against the things that moved in the night. 'The heartstone's beating like a drum.'

A dozen yards away, one of the shadows uncoiled in a fast, loping movement. Two pale eyes opened in the gloom, wide spaced and sickly yellow and instantly Jack had a flashback to the memory the Sky Queen had unlocked in his mind – shadow beasts with those same haunting eyes had pursued them through the dark towards the stone pillars. He'd only been a baby then, but the memory was clear and powerful.

Something moved out there. Another pair of eyes opened, headlights in the dark. Jack glimpsed a flash of what might have been teeth. The creature leapt over dead branches towards them, lithe as a cat, growling in whatever it had for a throat.

Jack tried to tell himself he must be imagining all of this, but the heartstone was vibrating fast on his chest and he knew they had to run, and run fast.

Sword out, he pulled Corriwen close.

'I think they'll try to surround us,' he said. He and Kerry still wore the boots Rune the Cluricaun had made for them in Eirinn, boots that lent them the speed they needed. But Corriwen didn't have that benefit. She'd been a captive when they'd met Rune.

'Get ready to run,' he said, sensing her nod in agreement.

'Take Corrie's arm,' he told Kerry. 'We need speed.'

Something moved in a slither of black. It was so close that Jack caught a gagging whiff of rotten meat. Kerry snatched up one of the bulrush torches and jammed it into the embers of their fire. It flared in a whoosh of flame and blazed a fiery arc as he swung it around. The shadows drew back.

'Now!' Jack cried, grabbing Corriwen's wrist. They raced

out of the clearing, heading back in the direction they had come.

They had barely run twenty paces when Jack realised something was wrong. They weren't going fast enough.

'The boots don't work here,' he gasped.

'My feet do!' Kerry yelled back at him. 'Just *run!*'

They sprinted, dodging looming trunks, aware all the time of the pursuit behind them, until they burst out of the trees and raced down the hill. They used the downslope to give them momentum, feet thudding, hearts pounding, gaining distance on the moving shadows. Some way ahead, under the red light of the strange moon, Jack could just make out a cluster of buildings. He veered towards it. Kerry and Corriwen saw it too, and followed close behind.

The chance of shelter gave them the added impetus they needed and in seconds the houses loomed ahead of them. There must be people here, Jack thought. They'll help us.

Twenty yards away from the nearest house, Kerry crashed through an unseen barrier and fell headlong. Jack grabbed him by the hood, pulled him to his feet and they dived between two cottages and along a narrow, cobbled street.

Behind them, Jack could hear the scrabbling of claws on the cobbles. He imagined a long, sinuous arm stretching out to grab and rip, but he pushed the thought away.

They scooted up the street, searching for somewhere to hide, but every door, every shutter was closed tight. There were no lights on anywhere, no sign of life at all.

Jack swung round a bend, dodging up a narrower alley. He saw a barn-like structure and made straight for it.

Luckily, the door wasn't locked and it crashed open. As soon as they were all inside, he turned and slammed the door shut. Corriwen groped for the cross-bar latch and wedged it home. It clicked into the wooden slot, just as something hit the door hard enough to send splinters flying. They stood together, hardly daring to breathe while the thing scratched and growled in the darkness outside. Then, after what seemed like an age, they heard it move away.

Jack let out a deep breath.

'I think it's gone.'

Somewhere in the distance a baby cried. A child's wail rang through the darkness. A man's angry voice silenced it and then all was quiet.

'I don't want to meet those things again,' Kerry said. 'I'm staying awake for sure.'

And he was still awake in the morning when the villagers came and seized them.

THREE

The red glow drained from the sky and real darkness fell. Nothing stirred in the village. In the barn, Jack, Kerry and Corriwen huddled together, listening intently, but all they heard was the faint squeak of a mouse deep in the hay, and their own quiet breathing.

An hour later, the first glimmer of dawn broke, sending rays of light through the narrow cracks on the barn wall, real daylight now, to Jack's relief, not the poisonous glow of the bale moon.

All three were tired from lack of sleep as they roused themselves, stretching stiff joints, when sounds outside told them the village was waking up. Warily, they edged towards the wall and Jack put an eye to a crack. In the street, men were gathering, talking loudly amongst themselves. A group ran up an alley and came back with a piece of broken branch. Then the shouting started. One big man came along with two small dogs on a leash. They snuffled around in the alley then began to bark, dragging their handler across the cobbles straight to the barn.

'We'd better go say hello,' Kerry said. 'If it wasn't for this place, we'd have been up the creek with a hole in the boat and no paddle.'

No sooner were the words out of his mouth when the barn door almost fell off its hinges, and half a dozen men came barging in. Jack stood up on the hay bales and one of the men cried out in alarm before the rest of them rushed forward and grabbed him.

'Hey!' Kerry shouted, as Jack struggled in their clutches. 'There's no call for ...' A hand clamped over his mouth and he was hauled off his feet.

Corriwen twisted and kicked as two brawny men dragged her from the hay, but to no avail. These were big farming types, dressed in leathers and rough plaids. The three of them had no chance.

'Bring them out,' one man growled. He snatched Jack's jerkin and pulled him forward.

'You brought the nightshades,' he snarled. 'Let them in, you did. You'll pay for that.'

'We didn't bring anything,' Jack began, but before he could finish a big hand had covered his mouth.

'Save it, trespasser. You cost us dear.'

And with that the three of them were bundled out of the barn and frogmarched up the street, while men, women and children watched them go by, with sullen, angry eyes.

Corriwen managed to pull free enough to speak.

'You've made a mistake. We didn't bring these things. They hunted us.'

'Aye, and you broke the Rowan Ring,' the big man spat. 'Here and at the coppice. You must know the penalty for that.'

Kerry managed to get a breath. 'We don't know anything. We've just arrived here. We don't even know where *here* is.'

He grimaced at Jack. 'And here was I thinking this place was pretty cool.'

They were hauled to a big wooden building which Jack assumed must be some kind of meeting hall. The villagers crowded in as Jack, Kerry and Corriwen were shoved towards a stout table. From behind it a squat, bearded man glared at them.

'What are they?' he asked. 'Dwarves or sprites?' He pointed at Jack. 'You, boy. What's your ilk and where from?'

'I'm Jack Flint, from Scotland.'

'Never heard of you, nor your Scotland either, and I know everybody in these parts.'

He banged a hand on the table. 'I bring this testing to order. Three strangers stand accused. Who speaks against them?'

'I do, Master Boru.' A woman came forward. She bore a wicker basket and laid it on the table, opened its lid and drew out a brown speckled egg which she cracked open. Something grey and leathery rolled out. Huge red eyes slowly opened and the beak gaped, showing two lines of tiny sharp teeth. The creature looked more lizard than chicken.

'They brought the nightshades,' the woman said. 'And now my chickens are sprite-sick.'

A thin man came forward. 'They broke the sacred Rowan Ring. Not a nut or fruit left on a tree.'

Jack stood up straight, as tall as he could get, and still felt small against the men who surrounded them.

'Don't we get a chance to speak?'

'You get a chance to answer what you're asked,' Boru said. He delved under the table and drew out Jack's long sword. Corriwen's knives, the bow and Kerry's short-sword followed suit. Jack gasped when he saw the heartstone join them on the table. He hadn't even felt them take it in the struggle.

'Now, where, I'm wondering, would you get blades as good as this?' Boru asked. 'Not around here, I'm sure of that. No man but hold-keepers may carry such. They are forfeit.'

'They're ours,' Kerry said. 'You've no right.'

'I'll be the judge of who owns what,' Boru growled. He raised Jack's sword, admiring the fine blade. He ran a thumb down an edge, then started back when a thin trickle of blood ran down to his wrist.

'Sorcery wrought, for sure,' he declared. 'I've never seen its match. This was either stolen or bought for service to the dark.'

He glared across at them. 'You come here and break the Rowan Ring and come armed with sorceren blades. And we don't even know what you are.'

'We're people,' Jack said. 'People like you.'

'Ha. So you say,' the headman rasped. 'None travel

Uaine under the bale-moon. None but the demon-touched.' He jabbed a finger at Jack. 'Or the fiend-friend.'

'They hunted us,' Jack protested. 'We just ran for shelter.'

'I say you're outlanders,' Boru retorted. 'Outlanders come for mischief.'

'We're nothing of the sort . . .' Corriwen began to protest. But Boru snatched up the heartstone on its chain and raised it high. People gasped and made signs with their hands.

'Black heart! Just like your own.'

A murmur of approval went round the hall. A voice called from the back.

'I say send them back to the pit they crawled from!'

All around them the crowd muttered consent. The headman stood. 'For breaking the Rowan Ring and bringing shades and sprites, there is but one penalty. Take them out and give them back to the dark.'

'What penalty?' Kerry demanded. 'We didn't do anything.'

But a hand clamped over his mouth again and they were dragged away, unable to fight or protest. The villagers followed their progress as they were half-carried, half-frogmarched out of the hamlet, up a narrow track to a small hill barely a mile from the village, where several stout wooden posts had been driven into the ground.

Their captors pushed them against the posts and tied their wrists securely behind them. That done, the villagers turned and went back down the track.

'I think we're in a real heap of trouble,' Kerry said, when they were alone.

'They are afraid,' Corriwen said. 'People were like that with Mandrake.'

Jack's heart felt as if it had sunk into his boots. Their weapons were gone, but worse than that, the *Book of Ways* was back in the village, and the head man now had the heartstone. They were completely defenceless. A long, uncomfortable day lay ahead of them. And after that, the night.

'There are circles everywhere,' Corriwen said. The boys followed her gaze and saw fertile fields and little orchards on the flatland at the bottom of the hill. Each field, each orchard and coppice was surrounded by a fragile fence of thin branches.

'Must be some sort of protection,' Jack said.

'From the nightshades,' Kerry added. 'We have to get ourselves out of here.'

He leaned out past Jack. 'Corrie, you don't happen to have a knife in your boot?'

She shook her head. 'Not even the clever little one Jack gave me.'

Corriwen twisted and turned against her bonds, though it was clear she'd never break them. Jack and Kerry did the same, but soon the rising heat of the day, combined with hunger and thirst, tired them out. They sagged despondently against the posts as morning became afternoon and then the shadows began to lengthen.

A scraping sound startled Jack out of his daze. He twisted round, half expecting to see some animal creeping towards him, but it was Corriwen who'd made the noise. She sucked in her breath and wriggled round until she was facing Jack and Kerry.

'I remembered Tig and Tag, the acrobats in Eirinn,' she said. 'They taught me a few things when we escaped from Wolfen Castle. I think we have a chance ... maybe.'

With that, she bent forward, leaning out from the post as far as the bindings would allow. Both boys heard her muscles and ligaments creak as she pressed them to the limit of endurance and Jack saw her face twist into a mask of concentration and effort.

'What's she doing?'

Jack shushed him to silence.

Corriwen's arms were now pointing directly behind her and Jack thought if she pushed any further, they might pop out of the sockets at her shoulders. Slowly she forced her body forward. Jack winced at the sound of tendons stretched to their limit, but Corriwen ignored her pain, and inch by inch, began to walk her feet backwards up the rough wood surface, her head almost touching the ground.

'Sun's nearly gone,' Kerry said anxiously. Above them, the moon was still silver, but they had seen that before and seen it change.

The dark came so quickly it took them by surprise, and again the weird green flash rolled across the sky.

'I can't ...' Corriwen wailed. 'I can't reach.'

Somewhere in the distance, something big and wild howled.

Corriwen moaned and Jack thought he heard a distinct snap. Then all of a sudden he saw her edge away from the post. She paused, gasping like an exhausted animal, and stood up.

Only now she was *facing* the stake. Somehow she had managed to loop herself through her own arms. Then she winked at him and Jack's heart began to pound as she began to shin up the post. It seemed to take forever.

'Yes!' They both heard her hiss of triumph when she finally got both hands over the top.

Closer now, the big animal howled again. A purple wave rolled across the face of the moon and as it had the previous night, it turned red, glaring down at them. *Bale moon.*

Corriwen slid down the post and ran across to Jack and Kerry. Her hands were still tied in front of her, and one shoulder was raised higher than the other, oddly askew. Jack knew she must have dislocated her shoulder to get free. She scrabbled about on the ground until she found a rough stone and began to saw at Jack's bindings.

'Do Kerry first,' he hissed.

'Don't be daft,' Kerry said. Corriwen ignored them and scraped away until Jack felt the rope break and he lurched forward. Instantly Corriwen was behind Kerry and sawing fast as the purple sky deepened to night and beyond the hill, the low moaning sound echoed through the dark. As Kerry's bindings broke, Jack grabbed the stone from Corriwen and sawed at the rope still tying her hands. Further out, they heard again the feral growling of nightshades on the hunt.

Kerry rubbed his wrists and then hugged Corriwen tight. She winced in pain, but bore with it. 'You're a genius,' he told her.

'Tell her in the morning,' Jack said, pulling him away. 'Now let's move.'

Dark shapes came slouching past the barricades round the fields at the base of the hill, and Jack, Kerry and Corriwen began to run. They ran for their lives.

FOUR

The smell of burning followed them as they ran from the nightshades. Ahead was a small stand of trees which would offer very little cover. Jack knew they couldn't keep running all night.

Yet they couldn't stop either, not in the open and unarmed, he thought, as they crested the hill and ran down the other side.

'We should go back to the village,' Kerry said.

'Why? There's no haven there,' Corriwen countered. She was hugging one elbow tight as she ran, obviously slowed by the pain.

'Save your breath,' Jack ordered. 'And keep running!'

He felt defenceless without the great sword and the heartstone. The sword had been a part of him since the first time he'd held it in Eirinn, when he'd stood alongside

Hedda the Scatha, facing the charging cavalry.

And the heartstone, his father's talisman, that had a power all of its own. The key to worlds.

As they raced down the far side of the hill they could hear the creatures behind, howling like hyenas over a kill. Hyenas would be bad enough, but the unearthly shadow shapes – the nightshades – were so unnatural, so fundamentally *wrong*, that it stirred the deepest terrors inside his mind.

He had been carried as a baby as the nightshades hounded his father through a forest. The recollection spurred a supernatural fear, one that he didn't want to face ever again.

Suddenly a truly savage howl shuddered the night, startling all three of them.

'What the freak is that?'

Jack didn't have the breath to respond. The howling soared high and then subsided into a vicious snarl. It sounded different from the hunting nightshades, but just as terrifying. Another blared, but this time even louder, closer. Much too close.

'Surrounding us,' Corriwen gasped. 'They're *fast*.'

From the corner of his eye, Jack thought he saw a pale shape running low and fast about a hundred yards away.

He swerved and Kerry and Corriwen followed. They found themselves running towards the edge of a thick forest.

'No way,' Kerry blurted. 'Not again!'

He tried to veer away. Jack understood why. They had

been in forests so often in other worlds, and in each one they'd been faced with appalling dangers.

Jack risked a glance behind him and saw more dark shadows creeping over the hill like a rising tide. They had no choice but to run for the trees. Jack grabbed Kerry's arm and swung him back.

The forest enfolded them in shadows and the three ran in the dark, hands outstretched as they went, careening into saplings and through tangles of fern.

Now the howling was really close. Something heavy crashed through undergrowth.

Spiderwebs caught at Corriwen's hair, parting with sinewy snaps. Ghostly moths whirred around their heads but they still pushed on, over a rise and then across a shallow stream.

Kerry bent and snatched up two heavy rocks. Jack scrabbled around for a stout branch and when his fingers found one, he heaved a sight of relief. It was not ideal, but at least it was something to fight with. He hoped.

There was every possibility that the nightshades just couldn't be fought. If the villagers barricaded themselves in at night and huddled, afraid, until dawn, how could three kids do better?

He pushed Corriwen ahead of him, aware of her ragged breathing, knowing she was hurt and tiring even faster than he was, but he made sure he and Kerry were between her and what was coming. They barged through the trees, tripping and sliding while thorns and splinters spiked their exposed skin.

The noise was so loud it caused them all to jump. Kerry

turned, a rock clasped in his raised hand. Something flitted between the trees. A flash of grey. It growled again, deep and throaty.

'It's getting ahead of us,' Jack guessed.

Kerry launched his rock at the fleeting shape, a good throw, but it missed the creature by a few feet and smacked against a trunk.

The animal snarled again, ferocious and hungry. Then, from their right, an almost identical growl told them there were two beasts, closing in from either side.

Just ahead, a massive tree blocked their way, but Jack pushed Corriwen towards it. They stumbled over tangled roots until they came up against a trunk as wide as a wagon.

Corriwen reached instinctively for her knives. Her fingers hooked on empty sheaths, and she hissed in anger and dismay.

Jack took a second to check out the tree. Thick branches grew from the trunk, low enough to reach.

'Let's get our backs to the tree,' he gasped, feeling as if his heart was stuck in his throat. 'They're closing in. I don't think Corrie can run any further.'

There was nothing for it but to face their attackers. At least it might give Corriwen a chance, and he owed her that, after all they'd been through together; after she'd willingly stepped through the gateway to stand by him. At least he could fight for her, he told himself. He leaned against the trunk and laced his fingers together, forming a stirrup.

'Climb, Corrie,' he urged. 'Maybe these things can't.'

She didn't hesitate. She got one foot in his hands and groaned with the effort and the sudden wrench of pain in her shoulder as he boosted her up to the first branch. Beside him, Kerry launched another stone. It crashed through the ferns and hit another tree with a gunshot crack.

'Missed again!'

'You next,' Jack said urgently. 'Come on, man! Before they get us.'

He braced his legs to take Kerry's weight when from above, Corriwen called down excitedly.

'There's a light! I can see it from here.'

'What is it?'

'It's a cottage. A woodsman's hut.'

The beasts were approaching more slowly now, stalking them. Jack saw a flicker of red as their eyes reflected shards of moonlight. They growled softly as they closed in.

Corriwen clambered down from above and Jack caught her with both hands.

'It *is* a cottage,' she repeated, excited. 'In a clearing. I think we can make it.'

Jack and Kerry rounded the tree and saw the winking light not far ahead of them. Corriwen ran towards it and they followed her, Kerry a couple of steps ahead of Jack, who kept a tight grip on his branch, the only weapon they now had, ready to defend them all.

The clearing opened abruptly before them, wide enough to let in moonlight, and Jack saw they were running across a carpet of moss and leaves towards the light in the cottage. The scent of woodsmoke drifting in the air told him somebody was home, and that spurred him on.

The gibbering sound of the nightshades had faded away, but the hunting beasts were now so close Jack could smell them. He whirled, branch raised, and saw them clearly for the first time, hackles raised in spikes and eyes drawn into slits. Long fangs showed in twin snarls. They looked like pale wolves.

Kerry snatched at his hood and pulled him along. The animals howled in unison and Jack needed no further urging.

Corriwen was ahead, silhouetted in the light from a small window. Grey smoke spiralled from a crooked chimney of the ramshackle cottage. The boys followed her as fast as they could, all the time fearing those sharp fangs might close on their necks.

The door was wooden, splintered in places. Corriwen hit it with all her weight, bounced, yelped in pain and fell backwards. She sprang up and hammered with the flat of her hand.

'Open up. Please open.'

On the edge of the clearing, the hounds, or wolves, snapped and snarled, but came no closer, and that alone made Jack's skin twitch.

If *they* were afraid to approach ...

The thought was immediately cut short when Corriwen pushed the door again and it swung open. Her momentum carried her forward, and them with her. All three landed in a heap inside.

'Close it quick!' Jack cried, trying to untangle himself.

Kerry clambered up and swung the door shut. Jack helped Corriwen to her feet and looked around.

The cottage was tiny, cramped and cluttered. Cobwebs festooned old rafters. A fire glowed in a grate and above the embers a black pot hung from chains. It bubbled in the heat, giving off a meaty aroma of stew.

On rickety shelves around the crooked walls, translucent jars of coloured glass held an assortment of creatures, magnified in the liquid they floated in. Frogs and toads, spiders and beetles, and bits of other things that none of them could identify. A rough-hewn table was covered with mixing bowls and grinders and a heavy carving knife was jammed point-first into the surface. More knives hung from hooks.

'I don't like this,' Kerry said, eying the array of knives. 'It's like a witch's den.'

'Better than out there,' Corriwen whispered. Jack thought she sounded more hopeful than confident, but said nothing. He took it all in, the weird creatures in the jars, the pot bubbling away, and wondered if they had escaped from one danger and into another. This place reminded him of Hansel and Gretel in a fairytale forest.

Then a hand reached past him, a hand with long thin fingers, stained bright scarlet, and touched Kerry on the shoulder.

Kerry let out a wail of fright as a hooded figure bent towards him.

'Please don't eat me!' he yelped.

A pair of shadowed eyes peered out from under a ragged black cowl.

'*Eat* you?' It was an old woman's voice. Grey hair hung down on either side of her face. 'What a *disgusting* thing to say!'

She pulled him closer, inspecting him. 'And besides, there's hardly a pick on you worth chewing on.'

Without turning, the woman spoke again. 'You might as well put that knife down, my dear. You could cut yourself.'

Very slowly Corriwen lowered the knife back to the table. She'd moved so fast that Jack hadn't even seen it.

'Now, young travellers,' the woman said. 'I think you've had quite a night of it, eh?'

FIVE

The old woman flipped back her hood, letting tangled grey hair spill over her shoulders. Jack's eyes were fixed on the scarlet stains on her hands. Her nails were blood red. He still gripped the branch in both hands, wondering how she'd got behind them, who she was, and mostly about those ominously red fingers.

She raised her eyebrows.

'And you, young man. Go put that log in the pile. Can't be wasting good firewood.'

With that she released Kerry's shoulder and swept fingers through her hair, pulling it back to knot it in a bun, which made her less dishevelled.

'Oh, where are my manners?' When she straightened up, she was tall and lean, with sharp features and lines around eyes that were so green they glimmered in the firelight. 'Come in, come in. Sit down.'

She gestured to some stools around the table. 'Bring them closer to the fire and warm yourselves. You look just about ready to drop.'

Kerry picked up two stools, keeping his eyes fixed warily on the woman. Jack took a third. As he carried it closer to the fireplace, he saw the little door ajar on its hinges. He hadn't heard it open, hadn't heard the woman's approach. She caught his glance and nodded slightly. The door slowly swung shut with a muffled thud, making Jack start.

Kerry and Corriwen exchanged glances. She had put the sharp knife down, but her right hand automatically hovered near the sheathes on her belt, even though they were empty.

'Oh, it's so nice to have visitors,' the woman said, smiling at them. 'Young visitors!'

Jack saw Kerry's look of apprehension. He felt the same.

'It's been such a long time since anybody bothered to come visit old Megrin and now here's three of you, all alone in the darkwood.'

When she smiled, wrinkles made big creases on her skin, deepened by the shadows.

'Not a good place to go stumbling when the sun's down. Yet here you all are.'

She shooed them forward. 'Go on, sit down and take the weight off your feet. You've come a long way.'

Further than she could imagine, Jack thought. But how could she know they'd been travelling?

Tentatively they sat while she bustled about on the other side of the room. A tall broom was angled against a wall. An ancient rocking chair swung back and forth as if she'd just got up from it, even though she hadn't been sitting.

'Simple fare is all I have,' she said, her back to them. 'But good food and sure to fatten you up.' She turned quickly and beamed at them.

Kerry looked at Jack nervously. *Fatten us!* He mouthed it silently. Jack got the message.

Maybe she was just an old woman, but there was something in the way she moved that made her seem somehow powerful, and maybe dangerous too. As she poured a thick liquid into three stone beakers, a faint scratching noise came from outside.

She opened a small shutter and two lithe white animals scurried in. They ran down the wall, landed on her hand and disappeared up her sleeve, fast as rats.

'Slink and Slither,' she said. 'Always up to mischief. You two been a-wandering, have you? Guide our new friends to our hideaway, did you?'

Now Jack looked wide-eyed at Kerry. Whatever had howled and snarled in the forest might have been pale, but they were hardly little polecats. They'd been big and fierce and they had hemmed them in on either side, forcing them in one direction ... straight towards the old woman's home.

Megrin deftly sliced a loaf of bread that smelled as if it was fresh from the oven. Despite his misgivings, Jack felt his mouth water and his stomach grumble.

'Go on, go on. Don't stand on ceremony,' she urged.

The three of them looked suspiciously at the food, each not quite sure what to do.

Before any of them could respond, the old woman was behind them, faster than anyone her age should have been able to move.

She bent over Corriwen and her long fingers stroked her cheek.

'All out of breath you are, my dear.' Corriwen tried to turn around, but the gnarled fingers of the other hand had latched on to her bad shoulder. Jack gauged the distance to the knives hanging on hooks, ready to move. He and Kerry were already on their feet.

'And you're all bent out of shape, are you not?'

The red-stained fingers trailed down Corriwen's cheek, on to her neck, then both hands were on her shoulders. They gripped tight, nails digging in hard. Corriwen yelped.

'Leave her alone . . .!' The words were out of Kerry's mouth before he could stop himself.

The fingers twisted and Corriwen groaned. Jack heard a loud *click* and then the old woman's hands moved back to cup Corriwen's cheeks again.

Corriwen let out a long shuddery sigh and Megrin beamed at her.

'Painful, I know, but better cruel to be kind to fix a wrenched socket.' The colour slowly crept back to Corriwen's face.

'Back together again, good as new,' Megrin said. 'Now,

first things first. And you might as well sit down and eat, for no harm will come to you under my roof.'

Corriwen gingerly rubbed the shoulder, then grinned. She nodded and sat back down. Jack breathed a sigh of relief.

'Brave girl,' the old woman said softly. 'Now, to introductions. I'm Megrin Willow of Foresthaven. I'm good with potions and simples and a few other things, and this is my place, my wildwood.'

Taking encouragement from Corriwen's nod, Jack took the lead and they introduced themselves.

'Now eat. There's no potions and you won't turn into frogs overnight, as some people fear. Don't worry, I'm used to that nonsense. Sit a while and fill yourselves. It's a long time until the dawn, and we have all sorts of matters to discover.'

She watched with satisfaction as they fell on the food until there was nothing left but crumbs, then hauled the big pot off the coals and ladled out a broth as thick as stew. They devoured that too.

'I was expecting you,' she said finally, when they'd eaten their fill. 'You're far, far from home ... and you have lost what you had, am I right?'

'How do you know?' Jack began.

She laughed, a high and tinkly giggle that made her sound much younger than she looked.

'Oh, some of us have a knack for knowing,' she said. She leaned forward and jutted a red finger at Jack. 'I saw you come through the gateway, of course. You first, and then your friends soon after. And I knew you'd come visiting, sure as day.'

'We were hunted,' Kerry said. 'There's *things* out there. Nightshades chasing us. And then we hid in a village, but they found us and tied us up. Out in the open.'

'And that's how this young darling hurt herself,' Megrin said. 'Quite the heroine, I think.'

'She sure is,' Kerry agreed, with feeling. 'Once, when we were in Eirinn, she ...'

Jack kicked his ankle. Once Kerry got talking it was hard to rein him in, and Jack needed to know more about this old woman before he told her anything about themselves or the other worlds they'd visited. Kerry shut up. Megrin seemed not to notice.

'Ah well, you've met the *Malahain*, and not for the first time, I imagine. The people here call them nightshades. Foul little imps they are. And you can see that all's not well in Uaine, not when the sun goes down.'

'The moon turns red and foul,' Corriwen said. 'Like ...' she pointed at Megrin's fingers. 'Like blood.'

Megrin raised both hands, saw the stains and burst into a peal of laughter.

'Blood? That's what you thought? No wonder you were all backward about coming forward! What did you think, that I'd butcher you in your boots?'

'Something like that,' Kerry said, still not quite sure she couldn't. Or wouldn't.

'Oh, don't be daft. I've never eaten a boy who didn't deserve it. Not for *weeks* anyway.'

Kerry's jaw dropped. Megrin's hand reached out and he cringed back. All she did was ruffle his hair.

'Oh, I'm just having my bit of fun, young man. No, my dear, you were a bit earlier than I expected. I was mixing a potion for a wife who's due tomorrow. She's afraid she might be imp-touched and her baby born a changeling. But that mixture does stain like stink, I can tell you.'

She rocked back again, still chuckling.

'Best laugh I've had in a long time,' she said, wiping a tear from her eye. 'And you,' she pointed at Kerry. '*Please don't eat me!*'

Megrin was off again, giggling so helplessly she began to cough and splutter until Jack found the nerve to stand and clap her on the back.

Kerry glared. 'It's all right for you, in here with the light. But we got chased by ghoullies, caught by nutcases and then hunted by ghoullies all over again. And then you come sneaking up with your hands all red.'

She howled with laughter again until tears streamed down both her cheeks.

'Oh, I needed that. A good laugh clears the cobwebs. And now, what was I saying?'

'When the sun goes down?' Corriwen prompted.

'Ah yes, so I was. Well, you've seen for yourselves. Things have come to a pretty pass and that's why I was waiting for you.'

'For us?' Jack leant forward. He didn't understand what she meant or why she might have been waiting for them.

'Of course. I've expected you for some time.' She stood up and beckoned them towards a narrow window. Outside, silver beams lanced down. Here in the clearing, the moon was no longer red and angry.

Megrin took a candle from the table, snuffed it out, and let the smoke drift up the clear window pane. In a few moments their reflections fogged out and the window grew opaque.

Then, despite the dark outside, they could see daylight. Sunlight. And the tall standing stones of the Farward Gate of Uaine.

'My window on the world,' Megrin said. 'I don't often leave Foresthaven. This allows me to see what's happening in the world. And what has happened before.'

She breathed on the glass, then scratched some curved lines on the condensation before using the heat of the candle to evaporate them.

This time the light was different. They watched fascinated as Jack hurtled out from the stones and stumbled to his knees on green grass. Seconds later, the air between the pillars twisted and spangled and Kerry and Corriwen came tumbling through and bowled him flat.

'It's been a while since a traveller came through that gate, and now here you are. Three of you. That means it's time to put on my own travelling cloak.'

At the mention of a traveller, Jack's heart thumped hard and a multitude of questions leapt into his mind. His father had been a traveller between the worlds. A Journeyman. Had she seen him? Did she know him?

Megrin held a finger to his lips before he could ask. She clasped Jack's arm and drew him closer to the fire. 'It's a long story,' she said. 'But we have the whole night ahead.'

SIX

'Thin places,' Megrin began.

Jack and Kerry exchanged surprised glances. Major Macbeth, Jack's guardian, had spoken of thin places on the first fateful night when their journey had begun. That night they had fled from the horde of nightshades and come tumbling through the Farward Gate to Temair.

Megrin smiled as if she had read their thoughts. Jack wasn't quite sure that she *hadn't*.

'Thin places,' she repeated. 'Where worlds meet. Where there's always the danger that evil things, things from dark worlds, will try to break through to bring their shadows with them. A battle that's been fought forever, and always will be, but I imagine you know all this already.'

Jack and Kerry both nodded tentatively. From what the

Major had told them, the thin places where worlds joined could sometimes let evil through. And in their travels, they had seen evil a-plenty. They waited for her to go on.

'The thin place on Uaine was breached some time ago, but we, the Geasan didn't know it then.'

'What's a Geasan?' Kerry asked.

'Oh, the council of enchanters. Those who know the old ways and keep them alive. We had our work cut out, believe you me. But the dark forces, and the nightshades they have unleashed in our Summerland, are gaining strength.

'And what we need now is another Journeyman,' Megrin said quietly. 'To do the Sky Queen's work and stand against those dark forces.'

Jack felt as though he'd been punched in the stomach. She looked him in the eye.

'Yes, Jack Flint. *Another* Journeyman. And that shouldn't surprise you.'

'I came to find my father,' he blurted, unable to hold back.

Now Megrin smiled, but there was sadness in her expression.

'You have come a long way, and I don't know if I can help you on that quest. Jonathan Flint, ah, there was a fine man.'

Jack's heart began to hammer. He bit his tongue, forcing himself to listen.

'I met him and his lady, Lauralen, many years ago. They came to the Summerland, deeply in love, to live a while on the edge of the sea where they could watch sunrise and sunset. It was a peaceful time.

'But then, oh then, came foolishness and ambition. Greed and envy, and the thin place in a man's mind was breached, and in came the darkness.'

'What happened to them?' Jack couldn't stop himself. It was the first time he had heard the name Lauralen. Could she be the mother he had never known?

'The Journeyman made it his quest to hold the breach. And for a time the evil was thwarted and held at bay. But then something happened, in a very dark place where even the Geasan cannot see, and Jonathan and his lady, they ...'

She paused, searching for the words. 'They were no more seen in Uaine.'

'Like, they vanished?' Kerry asked.

'They were never seen again. The Geasan-Eril, the enchanters' council have worked long and hard to find out why.'

'The lady,' Jack said almost unable to get the words out through the powerful emotions that flooded him. 'Lauralen? Was she my ...'

'Your mother? Oh, yes. I'm sure of that. You have her grace and your father's eyes.'

'But what happened? Who ... When ...?' Questions tumbled in a torrent. Megrin held a hand up.

'We'll get to that before dawn, Jack Flint. Now let me do the talking.'

Megrin sat back in her rocking chair and began to speak.

Her voice changed, became deeper and more serious than before:

For a long time, Uaine had been blessed with peace and harmony.

But as night follows day, darkness always opposes the light. In all worlds it has been so, ever since the beginning. Always, the dark seeks thin places where it can break and wreak its malice. The servants of the Sky Queen use what power they have to hold it at bay.

And when it does break through, the Journeyman is summoned. How, only the Sky Queen knows. She chooses a good man as her champion, and his quest is ever to turn back the dark and preserve the light.

Before he became Journeyman, Jonathan Flint travelled here many years before. A boy not much older than yourself, Jack, on a mission of his own. He came through the Farward Gate, searching for his friend, Thomas Lynn, a boy who had fallen into another world, who knows where. He had sought him in other worlds and would not give up. Perhaps that was why he was chosen.

Jack and Kerry exchanged another look. The story of Thomas Lynn who had disappeared in Cromwath Blackwood decades before, and then reappeared dreadfully injured and completely mad, was a local legend back home. Nobody really believed it was true.

Megrin continued:

When he returned with his lady, summer still ruled in Uaine. But not for long. The Copperplates of Uaine, long scattered and hidden, had fallen into the wrong hands, and now they have been put back together and used to open the dark way down.

The time has come to remedy that.

Kerry couldn't help himself. 'What are the Copperplates?'

'One and twenty leaves of a great book, each hidden and protected by a *geas*, a powerful spell. One and twenty enchantments woven by a Geasan in ages long past, the enchantments that together brought peace and plenty to Uaine.'

'So somebody's nicked them?'

She raised her eyebrows in question.

'Swiped ... I mean *stolen* them.'

'A good guess, Kerry Malone. Someone has indeed ... er, *swiped* them. The Journeyman took on the quest of bringing them back after night-stalkers brought their mischief. Now Uaine lives in terror of the darkness, and that darkness is spreading ever wider. We fear it will flow over the whole world like a tide.'

'So why can't you get these Copperplates back?' Corriwen asked.

'Oh, don't think we haven't tried. But the one who found them, and brought them together, he was the most powerful Geasan of us all. Except for one.'

'Like a warlock?'

'A spellmaker, spellbinder. The seventh son of a seventh son. Once a good man too, but turned and twisted by the power of the Copperplates to dark thoughts and darker ways. I do know, for I'm the seventh daughter of a seventh daughter. And he is my brother.'

She sat back and swept her gaze over all three, expecting more questions but they waited for her to speak.

'Now here you travellers are.'

'I came to find my father,' Jack said, trying to explain that he had plans of his own, plans that didn't involve Copperplates or spellbinders or anything else. Yet, somehow, he knew he was about to get sucked into this world's affairs. *The Book of Ways* had made it clear that he had to pay his passage.

'And we came to help him,' Corriwen said.

'Yeah,' Kerry pitched in. 'All for one and each for everybody else.'

'A good sentiment,' Megrin said. 'Three friends good and true. And on a quest.'

'We have to go west,' Kerry blurted. 'The *Book of Ways* said ...' He looked at Jack, wondering if he'd said too much, but Jack didn't bother trying to hush him up.

'But we lost it,' Corriwen broke in. 'It guides us and they stole it. And our swords.'

'And something else?' Megrin asked gently.

Jack nodded. 'My father's heartstone.'

'Ah, the fairyglass heart. I wondered if it would come back. And if it's here, then all is not lost. Not by a long way. Not that it's going to be easy, mind. But that's for tomorrow and the days to come.

'Now I've done my share of talking, it's your turn. I want to hear your story.'

Jack began to talk, describing the night of the Halloween party when the creeping dark had swallowed Billy Robbins and hunted them through the passageways under the Major's house to Cromwath Blackwood and through the ring of standing stones to Temair.

'Then we met Corrie,' Kerry said. 'And she was in big trouble.'

They couldn't stop Jack as he told how they'd fled across Temair, stalked by creatures he had only read about in legends, the final apocalyptic clash with the Morrigan, then the perils when they found themselves in Eirinn.

'And then,' Jack said. 'I came here to search for my father. I told them to stay behind, because if my father couldn't make it back, then there had to be something stopping him, something dangerous.'

He tried to frown, but couldn't.

'But they followed me through and next thing we know is there's things chasing us in the dark and then the villagers caught us and stole the heartstone and our weapons.'

'And the *Book of Ways*,' Corriwen said. 'They said we were evil and tied us up for the nightshades.'

Jack looked at Megrin. 'I *have* to get the heart back, and the *Book of Ways*. And I want the sword that Hedda the Scatha made. If I find my father, he can use it.'

'If.' Megrin shook her head and got up from her chair. 'I think you should get a night's rest by the fire. You've had a hard day.' She laid down thick reed mats near the hearth and began to douse the oil-lamp wicks.

'Get some sleep and give me some quiet time to think. I have a birthing to attend in the early hours. We'll talk after that.'

She disappeared silently. Jack, Kerry and Corriwen settled down wearily to rest. Very soon they were asleep by the glow of embers.

SEVEN

Jack woke early from vague dreams where he hunted shadows. Kerry snored lightly, curled up beside the hearth. Corrie smiled in her sleep, hugging herself tight. Jack wondered what she was dreaming of. He could feel her breath on his cheek.

In the quiet of the dawn he thought about what Megrin had told him. His father had been here – might still be. But first, Jack knew he had to recover the heartstone. It was the key to all worlds, and somehow Jack knew it was also the key in the search for his father.

Kerry snorted and woke with a start. He looked around, bewildered for a moment, then got up and went straight for the cooking pot to help himself to a ladle of broth.

'Where's the wicked witch of the west?'

Corriwen stirred, stretched and got up slowly. They breakfasted while they talked about their next move. Jack was adamant.

'I'm not going anywhere without what they stole.'

'It won't be easy getting it back,' Kerry said.

'Nothing's ever easy,' Corriwen said thoughtfully. 'But we have met worse difficulties. They might be many, but they are not fighters.'

'They've got the weapons,' Kerry countered.

'Then we make our own,' Jack said. 'We got Corriwen out of Wolfen Castle, remember? We could sneak into the village.'

'Rune's boots had magic then,' Kerry argued.

Corrie clapped him on the shoulder. 'If you don't want to come ...' she teased.

Kerry's face went scarlet. 'I never said I wasn't coming! I was just pointing out that ... oh, never mind. All for one and that stuff, right?'

By mid-morning, when Megrin had not appeared, they set out on their own.

In daylight the forest was a haven of sun-dappled glades, a far cry from the threatening shadowed place it had been at night. They searched around a sapling grove for material to use for weapons. Kerry found three smooth stones in the stream and worked carefully to bind them together. Jack had seen him weave fish-traps and snares back home but it still amazed him how clever and deft he could be. In less than fifteen minutes Kerry held up the stones for inspection, each dangling from a stout braid of twine. They clacked together.

'It's what Connor used. Can't remember what he called it, but it works a treat.' He grinned. 'Although I still wish I had my sling.'

Jack was working on his own weapon, bending a piece of ash-wood into a curve. He already had four good arrows made from straight hazel, and although he had nothing to tip them with, he whittled their ends into points. They might do some damage if they had to. Corriwen had borrowed a big knife and used it to cut a good length of timber for a staff. She left two stubs of branches at the forked end and cut the base into a point.

'Tooled up and ready for anything,' Kerry said, swinging his makeshift bolas.

'We might not need it,' Jack said hopefully. Corriwen spun her staff and said nothing at all, but she had a resolute look in her eye.

They moved out from the trees and into rolling pastures. As they passed the first coppice into which they had fled, Jack saw the trees there were in a sorry state. Leaves wilted, infested with galls and mildew. The smell of rot was rank on the air.

'Did we do that?' Kerry asked.

'Not us,' Jack said. 'We didn't know about the barriers, but they seem to work. These nightshades, I don't want them touching any of us.'

'At least we know how to protect ourselves,' Corriwen

said. 'We should carry rowan with us always.'

'And hopefully it works on humans,' Kerry added.

They made their way carefully until they came to a hill from which they could see the village. Everything seemed peaceful and quiet.

'We should find somewhere to hide,' Jack suggested, 'then sneak in tonight.'

'How will we find our stuff?' Kerry asked.

'We scout around for the head man. He's got our weapons.'

Silently they sneaked down the hill in single file, pushed through a hedgerow and were halfway across the field when a man's voice bawled out.

Two men came clambering over a gate, big farming types. One had a long-handled spade, and the other a hooked blade on a pole. It looked like some kind of harvesting tool.

The three of them tried to make a dash for cover, but too late.

'It's them fiend-friends!' one farmer cried. 'They lived the night.'

'So much for the element of surprise,' Jack muttered. The villagers raised their tools and came charging at them. Flight was the only option.

A gate at the far side offered the easiest way out. Jack started towards it. Kerry and Corriwen sped past him in a blur, running so fast they were across the field in the blink of an eye. Jack followed, now aware that whatever magic Rune had woven into his boots was working again.

'What happened?' Corriwen seemed bewildered. 'I was ... all of a sudden ... here.'

'Rune's boots!' Kerry jumped up and down. The charging farmers were on the far side of the field. 'The old girl must have fixed them. Magicked them back.'

'But Rune didn't make a pair for me.'

'Maybe she did something to yours too,' Jack said.

'Good old her, then.' Kerry's grin was truly ear to ear. 'This is totally brilliant.'

They climbed the gate into a farm lane and headed downhill. But the cries of pursuit brought other field hands running and soon a mob was in full hue and cry. Despite their new-found speed, Jack knew they were trapped on the lane between the hedgerows. The only escape from the mob would take them straight to the village.

The noise of pursuit attracted the rest of the villagers as Jack, Kerry and Corriwen came haring down the lane, with the angry farmers in loud, lumbering pursuit.

They skidded to a halt beside a pigpen. Somebody had left a scythe against the fence. Kerry snatched it up.

'Frying pan and fire spring to mind,' he said.

'Rock and hard place,' Jack added. He looked around for any avenue of escape and nothing seemed promising.

'I think we will have to fight,' Corriwen said.

Kerry looked at her, then at Jack. 'Terrific,' he muttered.

EIGHT

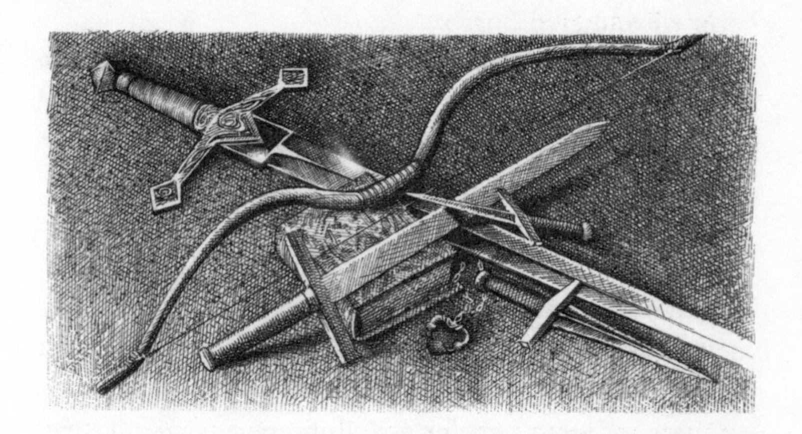

Boru, the head man, pushed forward through the crowd that had gathered, accompanied by several young men. He wore the Scatha's sword on his belt and walked with a swagger. The young men, clearly his sons, were each armed with the rest of their weapons: Kerry's sword, Jack's amberhorn bow and Corriwen's twin knives.

The other villagers made the evil-eye signs with their fingers and shrank back. Jack could hear them talk in stage whispers.

'How could they have lived the night?'

'They truly must be fiend-friend.'

'Demon-touched, I say. How else would they survive the nightshades?'

'Should have killed them first and fed them to their own.'

The boy armed with the amberhorn bow fixed an arrow and drew back. Jack stood firm. From where he stood, he could see the chief's son's aim was way off. He was no archer. Kerry swung the bolas slowly. Corriwen grasped her stave and eyed Boru's sons.

'Put down your arms,' Boru called out. 'You'll never get away alive.'

'Yeah, like you didn't already try to kill us last night!' Kerry's temper was rising already.

'We've come for our property,' Jack said. 'Give it back and we'll go away.'

Boru drew the Scatha's sword. Jack knew his father had wielded its twin with much more skill on Temair before Jack was born.

'These weapons are forfeit,' Boru said, swinging the great blade back and forth. 'And your lives are too.'

He took a step forward. His sons spread out to surround the little group.

Jack held up the ash bow. 'One move and your son gets an arrow in the eye. And for you, I'll send the nightshades. Nightshades that don't care about your rowan barrier.'

He turned slightly, gave Kerry a nod. Instantly Kerry understood. He wheeled away, whirling the spade around his head and raced along the barrier, slashing with the scythe at the upright posts. They splintered like matchwood all along the front of the village. A whole section of the rowan fence lay scattered.

The crowd let out a collective gasp. Kerry spun back and placed himself between Jack and Corriwen before anyone had time to react.

'Where's your protection now?' Jack asked. 'I swear I'll cut all of it before dark, and you'll never get it rebuilt in time.'

Kerry took Jack's lead: 'And I can conjure up even worse than that. You've never met the Scree, have you? Or the Fell Runners. And there's huge Cluricauns that'll suck your eyes out and roast your children.'

He waved the scythe theatrically. 'And they're all coming for you tonight!'

Corriwen suppressed a smile. She started doing a strange little strut, waving her fingers about and chanting in her own tongue.

'She's bringing out *day*shades,' Jack cried. 'They're even worse.'

The crowd fell back further, leaving Boru and his kin standing at the front.

'They're not getting this sword,' Boru growled through gritted teeth. 'I can sell it for two plough-horses at least.'

Some of the worried villagers protested.

'But if they bring the 'shades . . .'

'Not if they're dead, they won't!'

Jack watched as the men argued amongst themselves. The women looked scared. The chief held up the sword.

'You want this?' he challenged. 'You've no powers in the sunlight.' He turned to the strapping lad next to him. 'There's but three of them, with a scythe and a toy bow.'

'We can take them, Da,' his son replied. He wielded Kerry's short-sword, but it was clear he was not used to the weapon. The boy with the bow was still aiming off to Jack's left.

Jack pulled Kerry and Corriwen close and whispered to them. Now he knew they had one advantage that Boru didn't suspect. Kerry passed the scythe to him and began to swing his bolas. Jack stepped forward. His heart was beating fast, but he knew with the element of surprise gone there was nothing else for it. He had to have the firestone heart and the *Book of Ways*, the only inheritance he'd ever had from his father.

Boru also took a pace, a broad-shouldered Goliath compared to Jack's slight frame. He glanced contemptuously at the rustic tool.

'You think you can, strangeling?'

'I can try,' Jack said, trying to keep the tremor out of his voice. Whatever magic Megrin had wrought as they slept, they now had the speed they needed. Maybe that was all they had, but it might be enough. Jack crossed his fingers.

'Come on then,' Boru snarled. 'Let's see what you're made of. I'll fillet you where you stand.'

With that he let out a bellow and charged forward. Kerry darted off to the right in a streak of brown. The motion took Boru by surprise. He instinctively turned his head. Jack ducked under the swinging blade and jabbed hard with the back of the scythe. It caught Boru hard on the shin.

He roared in surprise and pain and Jack was past him in a flash. On his flank, Kerry was a blur of motion. Jack saw the three rocks of the bolas swing up and he heard a sound like a hammer-blow, then the big fellow who had Kerry's sword was down flat.

The sword was now in Kerry's own hand.

Boru hopped about on one leg, then spun very quickly. He grunted with the effort as he hacked wildly. Even as he ducked under the swing, Jack saw Corriwen sprint out on the other side and use her staff as a fulcrum. She leapt from the ground like a pole-vaulter and her heels caught two of Boru's sons each on the chin. Her knives went tumbling away as they staggered back. In an instant she was on her feet and both knives were hers again.

They might be outnumbered still, but the odds now were a little better.

The sword hissed past Jack's ear. Boru was in mid-turn. Without thinking, Jack thrust the scythe between his legs and pulled hard. Boru's feet came off the ground and he fell with a heavy thump.

The two sons gained their feet and hauled their father upright. Boru launched himself with a roar back into the fight, slashing and hacking wildly. Jack jinked left and right, forgetting about the other opponents as he dodged the swinging sword.

As if in slow motion, he caught the unmistakeable *twang* of a loosed bowstring. He was turning as he saw the arrow fly and realised he could not prevent himself spinning into its path.

Corriwen shrieked a warning, too late.

Boru roared like a bull and the great sword flashed in the sun as it whirled in his hands.

For an instant, everything froze in Jack's mind. The barb was coming straight for his chest. He braced himself for impact.

Then the Scatha's sword swung down in front of him. Right over his heart.

The deadly arrow hit the blade with a ring of metal and shattered. The lethal barb spun away and stuck into the earth.

Boru howled in surprise as the sword jerked out of his two-handed grip, whirred over his head and came down to land point-first between Jack's feet.

'Sorcery!' A voice from the crowd carried both awe and fear.

Jack grasped the hilt and held the sword high, sensing the power within it.

Nobody moved. A strange silence reigned for several minutes as Jack stood there, barely breathing, the blade poised.

He stared at his opponents. The boy with the bow very slowly put it down on the ground. Boru was bleeding from his shin and gingerly rubbing his hands together to ease the pain.

'You have seen what we can do,' Jack finally spoke up. 'We could do worse.'

'Yeah,' Kerry added. 'A whole lot worse.'

'Do you really want us to do worse?' Corriwen demanded.

A child sobbed in the crowd. A woman called out: 'No. Please. Just leave us alone.'

Jack kept his eyes fixed on Boru. 'Give us our belongings and we will go.'

'And no funny stuff,' Kerry said, brandishing his short-sword with obvious relish. 'Any tricks and we'll send the

Leprechauns tonight, and they're the worst of all. No kidding!'

Boru glowered, still wringing his hands and ignoring the wound on his shin. His eyes were fixed on the magnificent sword but he made no move to retrieve it.

He muttered to his nearest son, who turned back into the village. When he returned with their packs he put them down on the ground in front of them. Kerry and Corriwen snatched them up fast.

'A good decision,' she said, as Kerry checked their bags.

'The book's here,' he said, turning to leave.

'And the heart?' Jack asked urgently.

Before Kerry could reply a man's hoarse voice broke in:

'Fiend-friends in the daylight!'

NINE

The man strode in front of Boru, an apparition in a long tattered cloak, tangled hair hanging down his back. Around his head, a kind of hat woven from evergreen leaves sat like a crown and dangling from the ragged leathers he wore were small skulls of every sort, hawks and falcons, rabbits and stoats. On his chest a wildcat skull showed long thin fangs. He carried a long stave decorated with dried bird's claws and rabbit feet and other things Jack couldn't guess at.

'Who's that?' Kerry asked. 'The local scarecrow?'

'Or witch-doctor,' Jack said.

'You know the law, Boru,' the strange fellow rasped. 'They lived the night, which proves the rule,' he croaked. 'Kill them all!'

He saw the weapons in their hands.

'What's this? You gave them back?'

'No they didn't, rag-a-bones,' Kerry shot back. 'We took them. Any objections?'

Corriwen tried and failed to suppress a giggle.

A look of consternation passed across the man's face. He drew himself up to his full scrawny height. In the slight breeze they could smell cow dung and stale raw-hide. It wasn't pleasant.

He glared at Boru. 'I don't know what sorcery they worked on you, but it won't work on a spellcaster.'

He shrugged off the cloak and Jack saw the black heartstone gleaming on its chain at his neck.

'We came for the heart,' he said. 'Hand it over and we'll go away.'

The man's gnarled hand grabbed the heart tight. His knuckles went white.

'I feel its power, shade-bringer,' he cried. 'I will make use of it. What was yours is now mine.'

The man held up his skull-staff. 'Begone strangelings, before I cast a curse on you.'

'Do your worst, ragged arse,' Kerry cried. 'You couldn't scare a mouse. Come on, Jack, let's grab the heart and get out of here.'

He stepped forward; Jack and Corriwen did the same. The man held up the staff and began a low guttural chant, shaking the dry bones. As he did so, the air around them seemed to thicken, the way it had done in the Black Barrow on Temair before they came face to face with the nightmare of the Morrigan.

'What the heck …?' Kerry's voice sounded thick and glutinous.

Jack took another step and it felt as if he was wading in deep water. The great sword suddenly felt heavy and awkward. It was difficult to breathe. The air cloyed around him, weighing him down.

The ragged man's face began to waver as if seen through rough glass.

Jack saw a dark shape pass in front of him. It took him a second to recognise old Megrin in her black cowl and long shawl. She was bent with age and her fingers grasped a sturdy stick.

As soon as she appeared, the strange thickness in the air vanished. Jack finished his step, almost sprawling forward. Close by, he heard Kerry curse sincerely.

'A magician's trick,' Megrin said. 'Not bad for a beginner.'

The ragged man reeled back as if he'd been struck.

'It's Old Meg-o-the-woods.' A woman in the crowd broke a sudden silence.

'That was no trick, crone. I am Grisan here. The spellcaster.'

'Grisan, eh,' Megrin cackled. 'And what's your name, son?'

His face swelled with anger. He raised his skull rattle and shook it vigorously. A hush went around the crowd yet again.

Megrin stepped towards him, unfazed.

'You better put that away before you do yourself a mischief. Can't have beginners playing about with earthy magic. Oh, and what's that smell? You never heard of washing?'

'Beginner? Me, a *beginner*? Who are you to call me a beginner, old woman? I am Riggon the spellcaster. I could turn you into a toad. Or worse.'

Megrin cackled again, this time with laughter. Somebody in the crowd giggled nervously.

'Turn me into a toad? I could do better than that. I could make you smell like a man and not reek like a pig in a sty. But it might be hard work. I've smelt dungheaps more fragrant.'

This time the laughter was more natural. It rippled through the gathering.

Riggon held up the heartstone on its chain. 'I'll use this,' he cried. 'It has power!'

He spun to face the villagers. It took a second for him to realise their eyes were fixed behind him. He turned back and his eyes opened so wide they could have popped out.

Around Megrin's feet, grass, twigs and leaves were spinning off the ground. A sudden wind moaned, whipping her tattered shawl and cowl.

Megrin straightened from her stooped posture. Jack felt Corriwen's hand grip his arm.

Riggon raised the heartstone and shook his charm-stick again.

But Megrin kept uncoiling until, finally, amazingly, she towered over the ragged shaman.

Her hood fell back and Kerry gasped in amazement when he saw her hair, once straggly and grey, now become long and straight and gleaming silver. Her tattered shawl flapped in the wind, shedding scraps of material until it was torn away. Now Megrin stood before them in a long cloak that shimmered like summer gossamer, with a fur hood of pure white.

The old gnarled stick in her hand was now a slender carved staff, as tall as Megrin herself, and richly polished.

The shaman's feet seemed welded to the ground, his mouth opening and closing wordlessly.

Megrin turned to Jack who was flanked by Kerry and Corriwen. She winked at them.

She fixed Riggon with her emerald eyes. She didn't move, but in an instant he was squealing in pain as the fingers of his hand began to smoke and melt.

He fell to the ground and his hand jerked up. The heartstone flew up into the air.

Two pale shapes plummeted down. Jack heard a whirr of feathers as a pair of white goshawks snatched the heartstone's chain from the air, banked their wings and soared towards him. Their talons opened and the heartstone was softly draped around his neck.

He felt whole again.

'Neat. Absolutely neat, man,' Kerry said, to nobody in particular. Corriwen still held Jack's wrist.

Megrin stood tall and silent, silver hair catching the sunlight. Riggon got to his feet, his right hand hooked into a claw.

'Witch woman!' He backed away from her, still shaking the skulls in her direction.

She swept her gaze over the crowd of villagers. 'Some

of you know me. The old ones. Your mothers knew me. I am Megrin Willow of Foresthaven.

'And I am the Geasan, who has watched over you since before your father's father's father was a child. The Geasan always keep watch.'

She put her hands on her hips and shook her head, like an exasperated mother scolding children.

'You should have come to me before, rather than listen to the prattle of this prancing pile of rags.' She tossed her hair contemptuously. 'This will keep the shades at bay a while.' Her right hand came up and pointed directly at the shaman yet again. 'Root and grow. Root and *branch*.'

Riggon stopped dead. He looked down at his feet and as he did, a small boy in the crowd pointed.

'His hat, Ma. See his hat!'

Riggon stood paralysed. For a moment, the hat of twisted rowan fronds seemed to have turned into a circlet of writhing snakes but then it became clear that the woven twigs were sending out new shoots. In an instant, they had covered Riggon's face, except for his gaping eyes, then grew down in thin tendrils, over his shoulders, wrapping around and along his arms, and snaking round the stick and its skulls.

As all eyes watched, his toes elongated like burrowing worms and drilled themselves between the blades of grass and pebbles, forcing the surface to heave and clump as they rooted themselves deep.

His outstretched arms, encased in leaves, were flung out on either side, expanding as they reached for the edges of rowan barrier that had encircled the village.

As soon as the green leaves touched the first upright, new buds swelled up its entire length, burst and let bright springtime leaves unfurl and the magic continued along the crosspiece, down the other post. The slender barrier of branches took root and burst into life yard by yard until it completely surrounded the whole village.

Megrin finally lowered her hand. 'There, that should do it,' she said. Kerry couldn't help himself. He just started clapping his hands together in wild applause, watched by the terrified villagers who stood, mouths agape.

'Now you've got real protection,' said Megrin. 'A living wall, which the *shades* won't cross. And you won't need any amateur skull-shaking to keep you safe.'

She turned to leave, then faced them again. 'You did my young friends a great disservice. Think on that when travellers seek refuge and safety. Welcome them and succour them in days to come ... unless you want me to wither your rowan hedge.'

The crowd looked to Boru, expecting some response from their head man.

He coughed and shuffled forward. 'Yes, my lady. We will turn none away.'

With that, Megrin turned her head and walked away, summoning Jack, Corriwen and Kerry with a brief nod of her head.

'Come now, young friends. We have a meeting to attend and a long way to travel.'

TEN

Jack tugged at Megrin's sleeve when they caught up with her on the road heading west.

'Where are you going?' he asked.

'With you, of course,' she replied. 'Don't you have a quest?'

'You don't have to come with us. We know which way to go.' Jack didn't want to sound ungrateful for her help, but he was reluctant to draw anyone else into his search. Already Kerry and Corriwen had faced dangers on his behalf.

'Ah,' Megrin responded. 'Will you know what to do when you get there?'

She stopped on the road and looked into his eyes. 'You will be a good Journeyman, Jack Flint, and a good Journeyman takes help when it's offered. We all do the Sky Queen's work.'

'I just want to find my father,' Jack said. 'I don't want anybody else to get hurt.'

Now Megrin smiled. 'Good for you. A nice thought. But your quest is more than you think. It is bound with Uaine's future and the righting of wrong. As is mine. Uaine is *my* world, and Bodron is *my* brother. I would not have you and Kerry and Corriwen face him without my help.'

She patted him on the shoulder. 'If you could find him, that is. He'll hide himself well.'

Before Jack could respond, Kerry interrupted.

'Are you just going to leave him like that?' he asked. 'The witchdoctor guy?'

Megrin turned. They were only a mile out from the village and the green barrier of trees could still be clearly seen.

'Oh, for a while anyway.' She smiled mischievously. 'This way he can do some good and no mischief.'

As they walked alongside her Jack noticed that the gossamer cloak and white fur hood were slowly darkening to the drab colours she had worn when they first met her. She was no longer bent like an old woman, and walked with a determined air, using her carved staff like a hiker. From the corner of his eye, Jack got the impression that she was skimming over the ground, rather than treading it.

'What's happened to your cloak?' Corriwen was curious.

Megrin smiled again. 'That was just for show, you know. But you wouldn't expect me to travel in my summer best, would you? I prefer to slip into something more comfortable.'

Jack marvelled at how quickly they covered distance. The farmland gave way to moor and then hills which rose ever steeper as the road carried them higher, until they were walking in low clouds. Here, the air was cold and damp and a wind had picked up, driving rain and sleet into their faces.

They were hungry and tired when Megrin finally called a halt. Jack saw they were on a windswept summit where three standing stones formed the legs of a colossal table, bearing a wide flat capstone in weather-worn granite. Beyond, where the sun was slowly sinking towards the horizon, the sky was a dark smudge, the same purple shade they had seen in the night.

Megrin herded them towards the shelter but Jack held back, eying the megalith with suspicion.

'Do you plan to brave the wind and sleet alone tonight?'

'I'm wary of standing stones,' he said. 'Every time we go through them we end up in trouble.'

'I'm with Jack on that,' Kerry said. Corriwen nodded her agreement.

Megrin chuckled, stooping to get under the capstone, and took her shawl off, letting her silver hair spill down her shoulders.

'That's the Faery Gates you're talking about. The gates *between.*' She beckoned them to join her. 'This is a *Bor-Dion,* as they say in the old tongue, a resting place carved from the hill and set here to shelter the weary.'

Jack stepped forward. As soon as he was under the capstone the wind died, although, beyond the massive pillars he could see tussock-grass and heather bent almost flat by its force. He allowed himself to relax and the cold began to seep out of his bones.

'They built well, the old people,' Megrin said. 'And cast their *geas* to ward off harm.'

'I'm just glad to be out of the freakin' weather,' Kerry said, slumping down on the dry earth beside a small circle of stones where previous travellers had lit a fire. 'It's like being back in Scotland home in winter. All drizzle and sleet.'

He looked at Jack. 'I'm frozen stiff. I thought this was supposed to be the Summerland!'

'Uaine *is* the Summerland,' Megrin interjected. 'But you know that all is not well here. The time has come to rectify that. If we can.'

Kerry set about gathering wind-blown leaves and twigs which he crumpled together in the old hearth. Corriwen shook the rain from her hair and laid her cloak out to dry.

'Where are we going?' Jack asked. 'And what are we supposed to do?'

Kerry flicked his little lighter to try to set the damp leaves alight. The flame flared out like a blowlamp and he yelped as it scorched his thumb.

'Why don't you consult that book of yours?' Megrin replied. 'It's led you on the right path so far.'

Jack wasn't surprised she knew the secret of the *Book of Ways.* There was a lot more to Megrin than he had first suspected. He squatted down and drew the ancient book from his satchel.

Kerry cursed under his breath and sucked his thumb, unable to set fire to the wet leaves. Megrin glanced across at him, frowned, then closed her eyes for a moment. She pointed a long finger at the unpromising pile of kindling and when she opened her eyes again, Jack saw them flash brightly for a mere fraction of a second.

Something whickered past him, an invisible twist in the air. He felt it hot on his cheek. The firewood burst into flame with a sudden *whoosh*.

Kerry jerked back with a cry of alarm and fell hard with his feet in the air, frantically rubbing at his eyes. He looked up at Megrin who still stood with her finger pointing.

'You've burnt my eyebrows right off,' he yelled. 'You could have blinded me!'

Corriwen burst into peals of laughter. As Kerry rolled on the ground she slumped against Jack, helpless with mirth. Tears streamed down her face and he felt her convulse against him. It was the first time in a long while that Jack had heard her really laugh.

Kerry pulled his hands away from his eyes, glared up at them: 'And what are you laughing at?'

Jack felt laughter bubble up inside him too, until his knees started to shake and he could take Corriwen's weight no longer. They sagged to the ground, holding on to each other.

'There's nothing funny in getting blinded,' Kerry snorted. 'Freakin' witchy magic!'

But that only set them off again until they were both knotted in a heap, unable to stop.

'A pair of kids, so you are,' Kerry said. 'We're supposed to be on serious business here!'

He looked up at Megrin who seemed to have caught the

laughter infection and couldn't help smiling. 'Next time you should give me some warning instead of blowing me to smithereens.'

'I'll try to remember, Master Kerry,' she said as she opened a little cloth bag and produced some of the bread and meat left over from the night before. 'Now, about that serious business …'

Jack held the *Book of Ways* in both hands as the leather cover opened slowly. When the flickering pages stopped, words began to appear on the blank page. Megrin leant over them as they huddled to read.

Road now leads to ring of power
Ever on to shadow glower
Heroes may be tested sore
Journeyman returns once more.

Heed the wise, yet follow heart
Journeyman must then depart
To face the weird of evil bane
Ever on to madness reign.

Jack let the book close in his hands. 'It doesn't look good,' he said.

'It never did before,' Corriwen said, as brightly as she could, but both Jack and Kerry could read her. She knew there was trouble ahead, but she was ready to meet it. 'And aren't we still whole?'

'I don't like this madness thing,' Kerry said. 'And I don't want to be tested sore again.'

Jack managed a smile. 'I told you to stay behind. This is *my* problem.'

'Ah, how much you must learn, Jack Flint,' Megrin interrupted. 'I saw you all come through the gate a long time ago. The three of you as one. There's power in the number, the unshakeable triangle.'

'It's like I keep telling them,' Kerry said. 'All for one and each for everybody else! But I still don't like this madness thing. Not one bit.'

Megrin ushered them round the fire and they sat around its glow, breaking off generous hunks of the meat and bread she'd carried in her pack. She waited patiently until they had eaten their fill. The fire would die down every now and again but she would gesture with her fingers and it would flare hot again. Kerry remained wary, but somehow he managed to anticipate her and pulled back from the hearth. Though she tried, Corriwen failed to hide a smile.

'This ring of power,' Jack said, thinking about what they had just read. 'It sounds like something in a book I once read. It was a magic ring that made you invisible. Do you know what the ring is?'

'I do,' Megrin said. 'And it is not the kind of ring that will fit your finger. It's our destination. I knew that before your book told you. It is where I am supposed to take you . . . first.'

'And then what?' Kerry wanted to know.

'Then, if you are still as determined as you seem to be, we will go into the unknown.'

'If it helps me find my father, I'll go anywhere,' Jack asserted. 'The book says 'the Journeyman returns once more.' So where he's gone, that's where I'm going.'

Without explanation, Corriwen gave Jack a quick, tight hug. 'And we're with you.'

'For sure,' Kerry agreed. 'Though I still don't like this madness stuff.'

'Well said, all three!' When Megrin smiled, she didn't look at all like an old woman.

It was warm and dry under their shelter, and the fire stayed hot in the hearth.

Outside, night fell quickly and the moon shone down on them, silvering the ancient stone pillars. But when Kerry stepped out of the shelter not long after sunset, he returned with a puzzled expression on his face.

'The moon's red again,' he said.

Jack and Corriwen looked up, exchanged glances, then turned to Kerry.

'I mean, out *there* it's gone all bloody. From in here it's just the same as usual.'

'The old stones protect us,' Megrin explained. She stood between two pillars and raised her hands to shoulder height in front of her. Jack thought he saw two white shapes flutter out into the dark, but couldn't be sure.

'A little extra protection won't go amiss,' she said. 'Now, it's time to rest, for we have a journey in the morning.'

She settled down, huddled herself into her cloak and became as still as stone. The three travellers crouched by the fire, tired, but unable to sleep yet. Corriwen sat and used her leather belt to strop her blades until they gleamed.

'I'm glad she's on our side,' Kerry said, nodding towards where Megrin was sitting. 'Gave me a fright at first, but she's pretty cool.'

'Apart from burning your eyebrows off,' Corriwen said, keeping her face straight.

Jack leant back against the pillar, absently cradling the heartstone in his hand, listening to them banter back and forth, and soon the voices faded and he fell into a sleep.

Jack jerked awake suddenly, his heart hammering. The heartstone throbbed. For a moment he was bewildered, unable to comprehend where he was. Kerry and Corriwen were huddled together by the fire, and Megrin was still a shadow.

Out in the dark, something growled, so low it felt like a tremble in the ground, and Jack's skin puckered down his spine. Slowly he eased himself round the pillar and looked out into the night.

The two wolves were back, white hackles bristling in

stiff quills, pacing a perimeter barely a hundred steps away from where Jack crouched.

Beyond, the night was dark, but reddened by a faint glow from the angry moon, and in its shadows, other shadows loped and squirmed in a heaving mass. Now and then, yellow eyes would flare in the dark.

The image of those eyes hunting him through the darkwood came back all of a sudden and he held tight to the heartstone.

But the white wolves padded back and forth, back and forth, silent as ghosts, and the nightshades came no closer.

Jack shrank back, wishing to see no more.

Megrin spoke in a whisper, and her voice startled him.

'This is just the beginning,' she said. 'We are on the far edge of what is to come. Worse things will face you.'

'That's what the *Book of Ways* said,' Jack murmured, his heart quailing at the thought of what might be worse than those terrifying things. 'It's never wrong.'

'And you still want to go on?'

'I *must* go on,' he replied. 'I've come this far.'

'You have a brave heart, Jack Flint. A Journeyman's son. A Journeyman now.'

The heartstone pulsed slowly and he laid his hand on the hilt of the Scatha's great sword. A small vibration ran through his nerves, and he felt comforted.

'Nothing can breach the *Bor-Dion*,' Megrin said. 'Not even the nightshades. And we are well guarded until morning.'

In the dark, she reached out and touched Jack's cheek. Her hand felt warm and soft. Like the hand of a mother, he thought, even though he had never known that touch. The thought made him ache inside, but the touch soothed him.

Soon he was fast asleep.

ELEVEN

'It's time to tell you more,' Megrin said. 'So you know what you might be up against.'

The morning was bright and clear as Jack, Kerry and Corriwen listened intently. The four travellers shared the last of the bread and meat, and drank clear water from an ice-cold rivulet, sitting around the hearth stones.

'My brother Bodron was once a good man,' Megrin said. 'And as adept a spellbinder as I ever knew. He was a leader among the council of enchanters, the Geasan-Eril. But if he had a flaw, it was that he wanted *more.*

'He was always seeking new ways, always wanting to be perfect, to be the *best.* As if being a Geasan is a contest, like wresting and racing. Nobody knows on whom the Sky Queen will bestow her gifts, nor why. The Geasan are what we are, and we do what we do.

'Ambition can become a thin place for the dark to break through, and I am afraid my brother Bodron's ambition developed a crack that grew ever wider under the force of dark tides. Through that fissure a shadow power slipped through to Uaine.

'As I told you, the Copperplates, the one and twenty great spells, were hidden after the great binding spell was complete. Together, they made Uaine the Summerland of peace and tranquillity. But for every good, there is an evil.

'Bodron kept secret his quest for the Copperplates, but he sought them all across Uaine.'

'I don't get it,' Kerry interrupted. 'If these spells made everything good, why would they have to be hidden? Wouldn't they make things better now?'

'So you might think,' Megrin agreed. 'But if I were to make a mixture of henbane and milkwort and a few other things, then it might help a woman who wants a child. Yet if I mix the ingredients in a different way, then I could make a poison that would kill a man dead. It is all in the *weave*. That's the way with great enchantments. Each has to fit with the other in the right way. Bring them together in other ways, and bad things can happen. And we of the Geasan fear the worst.'

'What would be the worst?' Corriwen asked.

'The worst would be if the Copperplate spells were woven in such a way that they would undo all the good they have done and open a way for dark forces to break through and cast an evil shadow over Uaine.'

Her face was suddenly filled with concern and sadness. 'I fear my brother has opened the Dark Way.'

'The Dark Way to where?'

'To the lands of the lost. The underworld. The realm of the damned.'

Some hours later, after a hard slog over rough hills they paused on a ridge. Far in the west, the sombre shadow swelled and contracted like a vast heart. Below the ridge, on a flat green plain, Jack saw a great circular structure standing alone.

It shimmered in a white mist, like an illusion.

As they descended, the image became more solid, condensing, until they could make out tall brown pillars, roofed in what looked like thick turf.

'What is that?' Kerry asked.

'Our destination ... for today,' Megrin said. She had declined to elaborate any further on what she had said in the morning about her brother and the Dark Way. They had covered a lot of ground, not stopping to rest at the other *Bor-Dion* shelters they had passed on their travels, and as they moved ever westwards, the heartstone's beat gathered strength. That told Jack they were getting closer to danger, but he didn't need the heartstone to tell him that. They all knew it.

They just didn't know exactly *what* the danger would be.

'I thought it might be,' Kerry said. 'But what *is* it?'

'It's where the Geasan-Eril sits.'

Corriwen nodded. 'The Council of Enchanters.'

‘So that’s what the book meant,’ Jack said. ‘Road now leads to ring of power.’

‘You mean that place is full of wizards and warlocks and the like?’ Kerry seemed to like that idea.

Megrin laughed. ‘Wait and find out, Kerry Malone. This is the first time the Geasan-Eril have met for a long time. What they – and we – decide will determine Uaine’s future. And yours.’

‘I could have guessed that,’ Jack said under his breath. Corriwen took his hand and held it tight as they walked towards the circle, not knowing what to expect or what they were supposed to do.

Jack could feel power radiate from the place. The heartstone now shivered against him. The hilt of the great sword tingled in his grip. The hairs on his arms stood on end and goosebumps tickled down his spine.

‘Do you feel it?’ Corriwen asked.

‘It’s like electricity pylons,’ Kerry said. Corriwen looked at him for an explanation, but she had come to accept there were things in their world she could never understand. ‘When you walk under them on a wet day you can hear them sizzle. It’s making my skin crawl. And one of my fillings is giving me toothache.’

‘It is magic,’ she said. ‘Real magic.’

‘Hey Jack, remember that big van de Graaff generator in school? The one that made your hair stand up . . .?’

Jack wasn't listening. His eyes followed Megrin. She seemed to glide over the grass of the plain and her ragged shawl and coat were changing once more, lightening in the sunshine. A half-smile played on her lips and her attention was focused on what was ahead of them.

'The power.' Corriwen pointed to the vast pillared circle. 'It's coming from there. And from Megrin too.'

It was only when they were within a few hundred yards that they saw this was no edifice, enchanted or otherwise, standing on the plain. It was indeed a ring, a ring of ancient trees, straight and tall, with bark as red as Scots pine and muscular roots dug deep into the earth. Branches high overhead tangled and twisted together so thickly that they formed an almost solid roof, save for a few places where tiny shafts of sunlight speared through.

Jack, Kerry and Corriwen marvelled at this living arena. Kerry reached to lay a hand on a buttressed root. Jack saw the bark flex and ripple and he jerked his hand back as if he'd been burned.

'It's alive,' he said. 'Like Sappeling Wood on Temair where we met the leprechauns.'

Megrin was ahead of them, now walking slowly, beyond the opening space. Jack followed her. She held her hand out to him and clasped his fingers.

'You feel the power,' she said. 'It called to me. This is home to me and mine. It welcomes you with kindness.'

'It's like Cromwath Blackwood,' Jack whispered. 'Much bigger when you're inside.'

Yet despite the tingling on his skin, Jack felt none of the kind of threat they had sensed inside the walled forest back home, when they had first run from the creeping dark and found themselves inside the ring of stones.

The heartstone was singing its soft note, but it seemed to resonate in harmony with this place, as if it too had found a home.

TWELVE

Under the spreading boughs the air shimmered like summer heat on a long road and Jack felt the sizzle and crackle of power like an electrical charge. Kerry's tousled hair stood on end. Corriwen sucked in her breath. Jack felt that inside-out sensation he got when they came through the Farward Gate.

As Megrin led them on, Jack thought he caught glimpses of shapes gliding in the dappled light between the vast trunks, but he couldn't be sure. Kerry had his head cocked to the side, as if listening.

Then a voice spoke softly in Jack's head.

Welcome, travellers. He stopped. Kerry and Corriwen did too.

'Who said that?' Kerry asked, looking around.

The shimmering air spangled with glittering pollen,

bright as fireflies. The golden particles swirled in magical eddies and coalesced into shapes that were at first gauzy and indistinct, but in moments, Jack could make out figures standing in a wide circle. As Megrin joined it, her skin seemed bathed in a mellow glow.

Kerry took a step forward, but Jack touched his arm and held him back. Something told him this was as far as they should go. He could see sparkling light ripple through Megrin's form.

'Megrin Willow,' the voice spoke once more. 'It has been a long wait, but we are one again.'

'Long enough,' Megrin said. Like the other voice, hers spoke inside Jack's head. 'But worth the wait.'

'You have brought the Journeyman.' It was a statement, not a question.

'The Journeyman, son of Jonathan Cullian Flint. Bearer of the faery-stone heart. And his heart-friends stand with him.'

'Welcome all.' The voice was neither male nor female, but it was gentle and warm. 'Welcome Jack Flint. Your father was ever a friend to Uaine. We owe you our gratitude and our aid.'

'We have kept the dark at bay as much as we are able,' Megrin said. 'Yet it spreads. What may follow may be the end for Uaine and all worlds. Now is the time to face it. To heal the breach.'

'We are as one on this,' the disembodied voice replied. 'The Copperplates have been usurped, their purpose corrupted. We sense that Bodron has unlocked the gate to the lost lands. Sooner or later, it will swing open, and then all will be lost.'

'I will guide them into Bodron's Domain,' Megrin said, 'and do what I can to stem my brother's will. Speed is of the essence now. I need to share the power of the Geasan, I need light to overcome the dark. And I need the Geasan-Eril to build a nether-way, to let us pass through the shadow-fields.'

She let her request sink in before she spoke again. 'This is a matter of destiny. The Journeyman and his friends are part of this quest. I will lead them to where they need to go, to Bodron's holdfast. And there I will face Bodron myself.'

'We cannot see beyond the dark. The future is clouded. Would you take these young travellers to their doom?'

'I *must* go,' Jack said aloud. He hadn't meant to speak, but some compulsion took over. 'My father went there and he never came back. I have to find him.'

'That we know, Journeyman. Your sorrows are ours. Yet there is a power in Bodron's holdfast that is greater than our own. Would you face it?'

'I must,' Jack repeated.

'And your companions?'

'Where Jack goes,' Corriwen spoke up, 'I go.'

'Me too,' Kerry said stoutly.

'So be it. You bear the Journeyman's heartstone. Pray it protects you.'

The voice faded to silence. Megrin still stood in the circle where the spangling lights wove around figures that seemed not quite solid, yet emanated so much power. She beckoned to Jack. Kerry and Corriwen followed him as he walked towards the circle. The magical light seemed to sizzle on his skin as he passed through the perimeter. They joined him at its centre, wide-eyed with wonder.

All around them, wise faces looked on them kindly, yet with sadness. The heartstone thrummed as it picked up the energy within the ring of spellbinders.

Megrin joined them. She raised her staff. Its carved head suddenly glowed with unearthly light.

'Open the way through the darkness,' she said aloud.

For a moment there was silence, followed by the soft hum of many voices in harmony, a harmony that swelled louder as it gained strength. Jack felt jolts of energy tingle on the nerves of his fingers and down his spine.

The air before them wavered, and a harsh ripping sound almost drowned out the voices. A space opened in the air, yawning dark, like the mouth of a tunnel.

The dust at their feet was sucked into what seemed like a black void, an emptiness so profound it hurt Jack's eyes to stare into it.

It was like a rip in the fabric of the world. An opening between this place and somewhere else: somewhere shadowed and bleak.

Jack knew that's exactly what it was.

Thin places. The words formed in his mind. *Between here and ... where?*

Megrin put her hand on Jack's shoulder and ushered them forward towards the opening. Corriwen gripped Jack's arm. Kerry looked transfixed and when Jack pulled him forward, his feet seemed glued to the ground. Jack tugged a little harder and Kerry followed dumbly.

Together they stepped inside and the sound of voices was abruptly cut off. The light vanished and they stood in a silent gloom.

THIRTEEN

They were in a tunnel. Its translucent walls pulsed rhythmically as if they were in the belly of some monstrous beast. Ahead darkness stretched into the distance.

Megrin strode ahead and Jack hurried to follow. The walls squeezed in on them, contracting in powerful rhythms, propelling them further and faster.

Corriwen caught a movement in her peripheral vision and when she turned she saw something, a shape beyond the outer surface of the tunnel. Kerry noticed it too and cringed away.

The creature loomed in and pressed itself against the pulsing wall. Jack saw a flat snout and a wide mouth, and then he almost lost his footing when it pushed against the yielding wall, stretching it inwards like a rubber membrane.

Jack pulled Corriwen away. The creature, whatever it was, drew back and the tunnel wall smoothed out again. Ahead of them, Megrin slowed her pace and waited for them to catch up. She drew them close.

'Whatever you see is . . . beyond,' she said. In the strange atmosphere of this place, her words seemed distant, struggling through the thin air. 'We have the protection of the Geasan. You can't come to harm here.'

'Not yet,' Corriwen said softy, though she did not seem afraid. She had faced danger before with courage and determination. Jack knew they would all need courage, because wherever this strange *between*-way led, they were sure to find danger at the far side.

'Always looking on the bright side, Corrie,' Kerry joked, managing to raise a smile. 'You could try to be optimistic for once.'

They forged ahead, down what seemed to be an endless wormhole until finally Jack became aware of a change in the air. The burning smell was faint at first, but it strengthened with every step they took until it began to make his eyes water and Kerry sneezed explosively.

Megrin halted abruptly and spread her arms to ensure they stayed behind her.

The far mouth of the tunnel yawned ahead of her. 'The end of the road,' she said.

They stepped out into a strange twilight filled with shadows. Behind them the mouth of the tunnel rolled around on itself. Megrin led them away from it and they watched as the opening abruptly contracted like the pupil of an eye and then the between-way vanished completely.

There was no way back. Jack stood for a moment, lost in his own thoughts. Somewhere ahead of them they would find Bodron and whatever had brought the nightshades to infest Uaine. There, Jack hoped, he would find the answers to his questions.

Yet he was all too aware that Kerry and Corriwen had followed him to stand at his side, and they were now his responsibility. This was his quest, not theirs. If they had put themselves on the line, then he would do everything in his power to protect them.

And danger *did* lie in wait for them. The heartstone told him that. It was vibrating so fast, Jack was afraid it might shatter.

They were on a winding road. Barren land, strewn with dry rocks stretched out on either side of them before it vanished in gloom. Overhead, a purple sky loomed heavy and oppressive. No stars twinkled, but a harsh red moon glared down, tinting the empty land in bloody hues.

Kerry shivered. 'Maybe that wormhole wasn't so bad after all.'

'Where are we?' Jack asked.

'Within Bodron's reach,' Megrin stated.

'It's a *bad* place,' Corriwen said. 'It makes my skin crawl.'

'And bound to get worse an' all,' Kerry added. 'Another fine mess you've got us into!'

Jack shot him a concerned look, but Kerry was smiling

his mischievous grin, one he used to disguise his fear and relieve the tension. He shrugged his shoulders.

'Just whistling past the graveyard,' he said. 'We've seen worse.'

'I don't know about that.' Corriwen shuddered now, and not from cold.

Megrin stopped beyond a curve where the road cut between two rocky outcrops.

And suddenly Jack saw it. Bodron's Keep.

It stood out like a wart; black stone towers cast long shadows; rugged battlements were set like teeth along a rim of cracked and fissured walls; slitted windows stared blindly out. Around the outer edge, a moat reflected the moon in streaks of red.

A single stone bridge spanned the moat. Even at this distance, the keep emanated such a sense of threat that it seemed alive and waiting. A line from a school play sprung to Jack's mind. S*omething wicked this way comes.*

Except they were heading towards the something wicked.

Kerry blew out between pursed lips, half sigh, half whistle. 'Well, it sure isn't Disneyworld.'

Jack struggled to force a smile. 'You got that right.'

'It looks *wicked.*' Corriwen's voice sounded thin. Jack shot her a glance of surprise. She'd used the very word he'd been thinking.

'Do we really have to go in there?' Jack wasn't sure if he'd spoken the words aloud, but every instinct made him want to turn back, find a way to daylight and sunshine. None of the others reacted and he was glad he had only thought it. He felt the profound evil within the place reach out for him.

They were all glad of the blue light that glowed on Megrin's carved staff as they followed the road towards the ancient walls. Darkness on either side hemmed them in. Jack was sure he could see things moving inside the shadows and, in his head, he thought he could hear the same kind of chittering he and Kerry had fled from on that Halloween night which now seemed so long ago. His hand stayed firmly on the hilt of his sword.

Shadows pressed them forward, until they were on the arch of the ancient bridge. Below them, the water was stagnant and slimy. It gave off a sickly smell.

'It's like the bogs in Eirinn,' Corriwen said, peering over the parapet.

'Worse than that. It stinks like the bogs in school,' Kerry said. He held thumb and fingers over his nose. 'When they're blocked up.'

Something moved under the surface. Kerry shrank back but whatever it was stayed hidden. In its wake, thick black bubbles expanded. They grew to the size of beach-balls and then, with faint liquid sounds, they broke from the surface and began to float up, first one, then three, then a dozen, wobbling as they rose.

'Creepy balloons,' Kerry said, shuddering. He raised the short-sword and touched the tip against the nearest one. It exploded with a loud *pop* and a swirl of green gas billowed out, twisting in the air.

Corriwen gave a cry of alarm.

Something that looked like a hand made out of vapour,

reached out like a striking snake. Fingers spread like talons, aiming straight at Corriwen's eyes.

'Jeez . . .!' Kerry gasped. He shouldered her aside, but not before the smoky claw drew itself across Corriwen's cheek. Three livid lines slanted down her skin to the corner of her mouth, as stark as new tattoos. She screwed her eyes tight and hissed in pain.

Corriwen groaned, one hand clapped to her injured cheek.

'It burns,' she gasped. 'But it's as cold as ice.'

Megrin was at Corriwen's side in an instant, her face filled with concern. She brought her staff closer and examined the lines in its glow.

'Bear with the hurt if you can until I can attend to that,' she said.

Corriwen nodded and pushed on, saying nothing. Jack and Kerry backed away from the edge as the writhing shapes spun silently in the thick air, crowding up from the water.

'What are these things?' Kerry's voice was tight.

'Illusion, that's all,' Megrin said. 'But their touch is cold enough to chill the soul . . . and freeze the heart.'

Jack pulled Kerry in towards the centre of the bridge. He glanced back and now he saw the darkness had crept as close as the edge of the moat.

'Move, now,' Megrin commanded. She raised her staff and held it high. Sapphire light blazed out and the dark shadow shrank back. The vaporous things faded like smoke in the wind.

'There's a *geas* on this place,' she said. 'A barrage-spell. This keep wants no visitors.'

'We guessed that,' Kerry said. 'No welcome mat, no flags.'

'There are bound to be more tricks,' Megrin added, but before she could continue, the bridge gave an almighty shudder. Heavy slabs on the parapet were thrown into the air and fell into the moat, sending up a foul-smelling spray.

'We should move,' Megrin said quickly.

'No kidding!'

Jack rapped his knuckles on the back of Kerry's head. 'Don't get smart ... just *move*.'

'At least one of you has sense.'

'Two of us,' Corriwen snorted. She grabbed Kerry's arm and dragged him along beside her.

The bridge lurched again. A crack zig-zagged its way between their feet and rippled up the centre of the bridge.

'Maybe we *should* move.' Kerry squirmed out of Corriwen's grip and took her hand. 'Come on,' he said. 'Race you to the other side.'

Megrin braced herself against the balustrade and looked down into the water and saw the ridged back of something scaly and powerful break the surface.

She muttered under her breath and reached into her cloak. Then, with a quick motion, shook the contents of a small pouch onto the water.

As they hit the surface, blue flames shot across the moat. A deep bellow echoed up from under the arch. Jack got a glimpse of toad-like eyes and a toothless mouth big enough to swallow a man. It bellowed again, then dived under the water and shot away along the moat, so fast that the water foamed and swamped over the banks. Megrin waited until it vanished in the gloom.

They moved quickly over the arch of the lurching bridge as cracks underfoot widened in a series of harsh fissures. Jack raced for the far side, in step with Kerry and Corriwen as the whole structure began to buckle.

Behind them, the water was now a wall of flames. More stonework slid off and then the bridge's back broke. It slumped down in two halves, before it subsided slowly into the water and disappeared.

'Looks like we've just burnt our bridge,' Kerry said.

FOURTEEN

The walls of Bodron's Keep loomed high, like sea-cliffs, reaching for the oppressive sky. Massive stone blocks, piled on one another, solid and set. Contorted ivy dug roots into cracks and grizzled the face in straggly growth.

A great bell tolled, an unearthly sound. It seemed to come from deep below their feet.

'Where's the door?' Kerry asked.

There was no door in the wall, even though the cobbled road from this side of the bridge led directly to it. Jack craned back to scan the battlements overhead. A narrow tower stretched even higher, and dark things flew around it. He couldn't tell if they were birds or bats, but they seemed too big to be either.

A motion high above caught his eye, but when he looked directly at where it had been, he could see nothing but shadows. He sensed a presence. Something examining him with cold malevolence. He shuddered. This place made him feel somehow contaminated. The heartstone shivered too.

Megrin approached the wall and held up her staff. Corriwen turned towards the moat, both knives ready, in case anything hauled itself out of the water where flames exploded the bubbles that burst where the bridge had stood.

Megrin closed her eyes and pressed one hand on the wall. Jack heard her mutter, though her words were incomprehensible.

He felt the ground shudder, sending ripples across the moat. Megrin spoke again, louder this time. Another shudder, and a grinding sound of stone on stone.

Jack stood beside Kerry and Corriwen and watched fascinated as the stonework ground apart, block by block, until a high arched entrance became clearly visible.

On either side, each curve arced up to a keystone carved into a skull. Beyond, a massive door studded with nails barred the way. A heavy knocker the size of a wreath was etched with grotesque faces, bulging eyes glinting in the half-light.

'How do we get in?' Kerry asked. 'Just knock?'

Megrin didn't respond. She raised the staff and slammed its end against the door. A loud creak split the air. Small puffs of rust erupted from massive hinges and very slowly, the door opened.

At first, Jack could see only darkness inside. He wrinkled his nose against the stale smell of rot. Yet as the darkness receded, faint lights appeared and gradually grew brighter until they could make out the flicker of torches on high walls.

Megrin held up one hand to let them know she wanted them to stay back.

'Don't believe what you see, or what you hear,' she said. 'This is no earthly place, that's for certain. We'd say it was *weird-bound*.'

'You got that right,' Kerry said. 'Weird's the word for it.'

'Wait here,' Megrin instructed, then walked slowly forward into a wide hall. Her footsteps, at first loud and echoing, faded to silence after just a few paces. She stopped, listening. They all strained to hear, tense and alert.

There was no sound, but Jack could sense a palpable threat. He could tell that Kerry and Corriwen felt something too. The air was still. Dust festooned cobwebs that hung like drapes. Except for the torches on the walls, the hall looked as if it had lain empty for years.

But it was not empty, Jack knew. Something waited here. Something old. Something hungry. Had his father really been here? Had he faced it?

Did he die here?

Jack pushed that thought away. This was no time for such thinking.

But I wish he was here with us, he thought, I really do. Jack had no real memory of his father, but he imagined him to be strong and wise and capable. Somebody who would show him the right thing to do.

Kerry spoke, and brought Jack back to the present.

'I don't like this place.' His voice was an octave higher than normal.

'Me neither,' Corriwen agreed. 'I wish we still had the bridge, just in case.'

The words were barely out of her mouth when they heard a rumbling growl close behind them. They spun as one, but whatever had made the noise remained hidden.

'I don't like the sound of that either,' Kerry said. 'Maybe we should go inside.'

'She wants us to wait,' Corriwen cautioned, gesturing towards Megrin.

Jack forced himself forward until he was under the carved skull. The torchlight sent wavering shadows snaking across the floor, casting a dozen thin silhouettes of Megrin behind her.

'Maybe it's okay,' Kerry said. His tone said he didn't believe it was.

Before Jack could reply, the air in front of them began to waver like a mirage and Megrin's shape blurred. To Jack's sudden alarm, she seemed to be growing fainter and fainter, until he could see the flickering lamps right through her. Her trail of shadows shrank and vanished.

'What the . . .?' He took a step forward.

Suddenly everything went dark.

'What happened?' Kerry's voice came from close to Jack's shoulder. 'Who turned the lights out?'

Jack heard the scrape of metal on leather and knew that Kerry had drawn his blade.

Corriwen's hand found his arm.

'She just vanished,' Jack said. 'And I can't see a thing.'

For a moment there was silence.

'Go in,' Corriwen said. 'Whatever's happened to her, she might need our help.'

She pushed Jack forward and followed on.

The air felt thick in his chest. It seemed to congeal around him and his lungs protested as he tried to draw breath. A sensation of drowning flooded him with panic. Kerry gasped, reached for him and clasped his arm.

'Can't breathe . . .'

Jack forced himself to take another step, but the thick air wrapped itself around him like a membrane. With a huge effort, he dragged his right hand up to the heartstone. Its familiar pulse beat in his palm. Kerry's voice faded to a faraway drone, but Corriwen's hand was still on his shoulder. The heartstone, or her touch, helped him summon the strength he needed.

He drew the great sword from its sheath and managed to raise the blade until it was upright in front of his eyes. As if moved by some benevolent guidance, he raised the heartstone and touched it to the obsidian gem at the base of the hilt.

There was a blinding flash and an electric sizzle that juddered through him. Suddenly they were all tumbling forward as the invisible barrier gave way.

Light stabbed Jack's eyes and he clenched them tight as he clattered, still gripping the sword, to the stone floor. Corriwen landed on top of him, slamming out what little breath he had in a painful *whoosh*. Kerry cursed eloquently, dropped his sword with a loud clang, and groped for Jack's arm.

'Can't see a thing!'

Jack slowly opened his eyes, letting them adjust to the glare.

Now he saw the hall was transformed. Thick candles flickered on the walls where tallow torches had hung before. A long table stretched from one end of the hall to the other. It was laden with plates and goblets, trenchers piled high with all sorts of food. A high-backed chair sat empty at the far end.

Of Megrin Willow, there was no sign.

'Maybe it's not such a bad place after all,' Kerry said, eyeing the food hungrily. He sounded relieved, even hopeful. 'Just look at that spread!'

He started forward, licking his lips, but Jack pulled him back.

'No,' he said. Kerry stopped, eyes fixed longingly on the abundance of food. 'We're not welcome here. It's a trick.'

'Where's Megrin?' Corriwen asked.

'I don't know. But she warned us not to believe what we see.' Jack pointed at the long table. 'That's a trick,' he repeated. 'It *wants* us to eat.'

It. Not Bodron. The presence on the battlements. Something told him it was not human.

'You think it's poisoned?'

'I don't know. But we daren't touch it.'

'It?'

'Whatever lurks here,' Corriwen said softly.

'Something is watching us,' Jack said, and Corriwen nodded agreement. All around them the high walls were festooned with old tapestries, depicting battlegrounds and hunting scenes. Carved stone gargoyles stared down at them from contorted, ugly faces. The aroma of cooked food was tantalising, but underneath it, Jack could smell something else, something mouldy and stale, that he couldn't quite identify.

Kerry jerked his head left and right. 'Don't say that. You're giving me even worse heeby-jeebies than I've already got.'

'Just let's be careful. I'd like to know where Megrin went.'

'Maybe she's found her brother,' Kerry said hopefully. 'Having tea and dunkin' biscuits and a nice old chinwag.'

'Maybe,' Jack said. 'But somehow I don't think she'd just up and leave us.'

At the far end of the hall, another arched doorway led out. Jack moved towards it, with Kerry and Corriwen very close behind, past the laden banqueting table, ignoring the goblets and the steaming trenchers. The meal was laid for a large gathering, but there was nobody here but them. It felt disturbingly wrong.

'Are we supposed to guess who's coming for dinner?'

Corriwen shushed Kerry. She knew he talked more when he was nervous. They were just past the host's high seat when the sensation of being watched came on so powerfully she turned mid stride. Jack heard her gasp.

He followed her gaze and started back with a sharp intake of breath. Kerry did exactly the same.

The gargoyles on the walls had *moved*. It was unmistakeable. When they had come in, the contorted creatures had all been facing them in the doorway, still as death, but grotesque all the same. Now they had swivelled to keep stony eyes glaring at them.

'Just a trick,' Kerry said. 'Has to be a trick, hasn't it? Some sort of clockwork? There's probably a switch behind the wall.'

He was talking too fast, and his voice had raised an octave again. In Kerry, that was scary enough.

'They're just stone,' Jack muttered, more in hope than certainty. 'They can't hurt us.'

But he kept his eyes fixed on them just the same as the three of them backed out of the door and swung it shut against those eyes.

Kerry sagged against the wall. 'I hate creepy stuff like that. Even if it is a trick.'

Now they were in some sort of dimly-lit antechamber, in which three smaller doors were set in the bare walls.

'Which way now?' Corriwen was pale.

'Good question.' In this place, Jack's keen sense of direction was no use. They had a choice of three. For no particular reason, he was drawn towards the middle door.

It opened into a long, unlit tunnel with a curved roof. Warily, Jack crept on, Corriwen and Kerry close behind, trying to make no sound as they groped their way down the narrow passage.

Then without warning, a powerful noise boomed out, like the beat of a monstrous heart.

Doom. Doom.

Not a heartbeat. Footsteps. Huge footsteps. The ground trembled again and the walls shook.

A low snarl echoed from the distance, deep as a fog-horn.

'Jeez . . .!' Kerry was backing off, tugging Corriwen with him. Jack followed and they ran back the way they had come.

Kerry barged through the door first, tumbled out, and rolled fast to his feet again. Jack pushed Corriwen past him then turned and slammed the door shut behind them as a mighty weight crashed against it. Little splinters shot out, but the timber held.

'Whatever that was,' Kerry said, 'I never want to see it.'

Behind the door, whatever it was snarled again and thudded angrily against it. They backed away, weapons out.

Corriwen cocked her head. 'I heard something else. What's that?'

The crashing on the door had been so loud that Jack had heard nothing, but when he turned to listen, another sound came clearly.

'It's back in the big room,' Kerry said, moving towards the door they had first come through.

And it was. The sound of men talking loudly and laughing. Kerry grinned, relief apparent on his face.

Before Jack could stop him, he was at the door, turning the latch, pushing it wide.

A banquet was in full swing. The previously empty benches were now crowded with men in leather jerkins and tall hats, quaffing from the goblets they had seen when they passed, laughing and shouting to one another across the table while they gorged themselves on food and drink.

Kerry actually drooled. Jack felt his own stomach rumble. But his mind was racing. The hall had been empty before. Now the table was crowded with men. What men? Bodron's men? Bodron's minions?

'You think we're invited?' Kerry asked.

As soon as he spoke, the roistering died. Every man at the table turned towards them. An uncomfortable silence stretched out. Then one of the men at the end of the table stood up, raised a goblet.

'We have guests,' he said. '*Young* guests.'

His fellows nodded and smiled, raising their own drinks in a sort of welcome.

Jack felt a familiar tingle ripple down his spine, as the heartstone pulsed hard. He held his arm out, to block Kerry, but there was no need. Kerry stopped dead in his tracks and Jack saw the hairs rise up on the back of his neck. His mouth opened and shut several times and no sound came out.

Jack heard the deep rumble of something colossal taking a slow breath. A gust of wind came from nowhere and snuffed out all the candles along one wall and in that moment the scene flickered and fragmented in front of their eyes. Then everything snapped into sudden clarity.

The man who had stood and raised his glass was no longer a man, but a warted creature with a flat face and bulging yellow eyes. In its hand – its *claw* – it held a dripping piece of raw meat. Beside it, a green nightmare with scales all over its face giggled madly.

But worse than this vision, something moved in the high-backed chair at the head of the table. Its back was to them, but they could hear its shuddering breath.

Jack saw two leathery wings began to unfold, very slowly, membranes stretched across long thin bones.

A coil like a thick snake wrapped the carved chair legs, ridged and shiny and ending in a barbed point. Jack felt his breath catch in his lungs and lock tight. He heard Corriwen whimper, a faint sound of fear. Kerry's throat clicked dryly as if he was choking.

The beast in the carved chair began to turn its head towards them.

'No ...' Kerry managed to get the word out. Jack was aware of Corriwen tugging at his belt. His knees felt weak and watery and he began to sag under the weight of the awful terror that ratcheted through him.

The face of a nightmare was turning towards him and somehow he knew with dread certainty that if he looked in that great dark eye the shock of it might stop his heart.

A scrapy voice commanded inside his head. *Look in my eyes.*

A paralysis of dread froze his muscles.

Then Corriwen jerked him backwards. Kerry was already running for the door. Corriwen followed but Jack felt a terrible compulsion to turn back and look into that dead eye and be lost forever. He forced himself to keep moving despite the gravity of the beast's will dragging on him.

It seemed to take him an eternity to reach the doorway. Then, without warning, the dreadful hold on him snapped and Jack catapulted through the door.

Suddenly he was falling; tumbling and rolling down a long flight of wooden steps, crashing, elbows and knees, shoulder and hip, down and down until he hit something solid and everything went black.

FIFTEEN

Kerry ran. He couldn't help it. The revellers at the table had *changed.* In a horrifying instant, the eyes that turned towards him had become pale and clouded, set in the bloated faces of the dead men he had seen when they stumbled through the slaughterfield of Temair.

Great black feathered wings unfolded on either side of the high-backed chair with a *schick-schick* sound until they stretched out on either side, and then the creature's head began to turn. All he saw was the shiny curve of a huge beak as it began to edge round the chair and he got a glimpse of a crater of an eye socket.

Roak, his mind cried, even if the word couldn't get past his dry throat. The carrion bird that had harried them from the battlefield and attacked them time and again, under the command of the dread Morrigan.

Kerry snatched Corriwen's arm and dragged her away, pushing her ahead of him. She went through the door and vanished. His own momentum carried him out and without warning the floor dropped away at an impossible angle.

He careered down the slope, unable to stop or slow himself as the floor curved down like a funnel towards shadows. Behind him, a rasping *caw* echoed in his ears and sent another shiver down his spine. He tripped, tumbled forward and landed on his shoulder with such a jolt that all his breath was punched out. He lay in pain, unable to catch his breath, while the dark all around him was spangled with little purple sparks that slowly faded.

Finally Kerry got himself to his hands and knees, whooping in great gulps until the dizziness passed and he was able to groan at the pain in his back and shoulder. He was kneeling on damp earth in a space not much wider than his shoulders. A faint light showed him roots poking through overhead, and a mass of cobwebs stretched like sails from floor to ceiling. Something with many legs scuttled over his fingers and he snatched them back.

Guilt washed over him. He had left Jack and somehow lost Corriwen, and that was worse, much worse than finding himself in this hole in the ground. He balled his hands into fists and pressed them against his temples in anger and frustration until reason began to take hold again. He had to find a way out of here and find them both. They needed him – that he was sure of.

Kerry drew the short-sword and began to slash his way

through the clinging cobwebs, ignoring the things that scuttled around his feet, not knowing where he was going, but relieved to be simply going.

Then a voice spoke in his ear making him jump so suddenly his head cracked on a gnarled root above and almost floored him.

Water comes, water goes, water rises, water flows ... It was almost a sing-song.

He twisted round, trying to find the source. But then he heard something else and his heart turned to stone.

It was the sound of running water. It was far off and distant and at first he thought the tunnel might lead to open air beside a river with a waterfall.

But there was something in that sound, something awfully familiar.

Not a waterfall ...

In an instant, he was back in the darkness under the Morrigan's black barrow on Temair, listening to the terrible roar of water rushing towards him.

'Oh, Jeez!'

Then he felt the walls shudder and a sudden punch of compressed air against his back as the crash of water soared to a crescendo.

And he was running, running in the dark, slashing through the cobwebs, hardly aware of the walls blurring past him and the roots slapping his head. Behind him, the flood snarled and bellowed, gaining on him.

Corriwen tumbled through the doorway. Kerry had snagged her sleeve and swung her ahead of him while the image of the thing in the high chair was still burned into her mind.

A peeling skull, mad eyes rolling in its sockets – impossible! Something in that glare had pierced to her soul with such foul intensity that she almost fainted.

The room tilted. Then Kerry had pushed her out and she'd tumbled through the doorway, spinning dizzily, flying into a grey nothingness.

Her stomach heaved and she felt nausea rise up to her throat as she flailed for balance. Miraculously, she landed on her feet and then stumbled forward and stopped, heart thudding.

It took her a few seconds to realise that the castle walls were gone; that there was no doorway, no slope, nothing at all. Nothing but a pearly mist that spread out around her in every direction.

She stood still, trying to take it in, to make some sense of it, to find something to focus her eyes on, but there was only a featureless sea of grey.

There was no sound except her own breathing and the beat of her heart. She took a step forward, feeling a spongy surface underfoot. If she made any noise, it was dampened to silence by the thick mist.

Isolation swamped her in this emptiness and awful silence. Jack and Kerry were not here. She couldn't sense them, as she had always been able to do before when she was in danger. Even as a prisoner in Eirinn she had been sure in the knowledge that they would come for her.

Something in her heart had told her they would come, and it had been right.

But how would they find her here?

Corriwen began to walk, picking any direction because they were all the same. She trudged on for what might have been hours, trying to find something, anything in the emptiness. The mist curled around her legs, but she was scared to stop and unable to sit and rest because then the mist would be over her head and she did not want that, not at all.

The further she walked, the more she feared she would be stuck in this grey place, alone, forever.

Some time later, a shiver down her spine told her that she was not alone.

Corriwen heard it, but she couldn't see it, and that was worst of all.

The mist had thickened and deepened and was now up to her waist. Then, in the heavy silence, she heard a sound, a low growl.

She turned in a full circle, spine tingling, trying to locate the sound, but there was nothing to be seen in the sea of grey. Both her knives were out and ready.

The growl became deep and guttural, too much like the bristleback boars the Scree ogres had sent to hunt her through the forests of Temair, but more savage than that. All she heard in it was a slavering hunger.

She backed away, hoping she was backing in the right direction, then she turned and ran, desperately searching for somewhere to hide.

The mist hid everything below waist level and she felt

like a swimmer in dangerous water, waiting for unseen jaws to open.

The creature grunted again, and she knew it was coming for her.

Panic swelled and Corriwen tried to force it down. She veered to the left, then to the right, trying to shake off her pursuer, but no matter how she turned, it was always within earshot. The mist did little to muffle that hungry growl. She knew that it would soon be on her and she would be fighting for her life.

Megrin closed her eyes and spoke in the old tongue, weaving a powerful command. A summoning.

In the middle of the great chamber, the air writhed, and grey smoke began to thicken and solidify into a gauzy staircase that led straight ahead, up and up until it vanished in the distance.

Footsteps, faint at first, grew steadily louder. She felt her heart quicken and commanded it to slow. This was time for resolve, not apprehension.

The slow treads gained strength and Megrin saw a shape appear high on the staircase.

He stopped, a man in a black cowl which hid his eyes and shadowed his face.

Bodron.

His breath was a slow, dry rasp as he descended. Bony knuckles tightened on a staff of black wood. He raised his head and she looked into eyes which seemed devoid of any humanity.

Those eyes were not her brother's eyes. They stared out from some hell where no light ever reached.

'Megrin,' Bodron spoke. Behind him, the strange staircase began to shimmer into the vapour from which it had emerged and it slowly vanished.

'Bodron, brother.' Her throat felt desert-dry. 'It has been a long time – too long to be alone in this place.'

'So you pay a visit. How ... sisterly. And what message have the Geasan-Eril sent you to deliver?'

The eyes fixed her with a black stare. His face was bloodless as marble and lined with deep creases. How, she wondered, did he know she had been sent?

As if he could read her thoughts Bodron spoke again. 'I have eyes in the night. They keep me well informed. So what does the council of spellbinders want of me?'

'They want you to put an end to this darkness. And they require you to give up the Copperplates.'

Bodron's sudden laugh echoed all round the chamber.

'I am on the far edge of Uaine here, far from the concerns of your spellbinders. Why should they interfere with my work?'

'Because your ... *work* is spreading out over the Summerland. Don't you know what is happening all over Uaine? Nightshades are loose in the dark, infesting field and forest, town and village.'

'Nightshades? Mere shadows. Surely your council fears no shadow.'

'It is what power brought them to Uaine that concerns us. What dark power have you raised from beneath and brought among us? The Copperplates have been turned to evil purpose. We shall have them, and we shall try to undo what damage you have wrought. Close the nether-gate you have unlocked.'

Bodron was silent for a moment. Then he chuckled, a low, cold sound.

'I spent a lifetime searching for these talismans,' he finally said. 'I found them. They are *mine*.'

'Not yours, brother. They belong to Uaine and always have, since the first great spellbinding.'

'Not great enough, obviously,' he sneered. 'Since I alone was able to gather them all and achieve for myself what took one and twenty of the greatest Geasan.'

'You were indeed a great spellbinder, Bodron. Why would you want more, when the power is a sacred gift from the Sky Queen?'

'Your Sky Queen is long gone from the worlds. She wields no power here. There are others as powerful as she ever was.'

'But why would you want to interfere with the good of Uaine?'

'What do I care for Uaine? I have more pressing matters.' He paused, and then his voice changed, just enough to give Megrin the merest hint of the person that used to be her brother. 'I *needed* the Copperplates.'

Bodron's mouth snapped shut, as if he wanted to bite back the words. His frame shook violently and he doubled over. He gasped as if in pain and then slowly unfolded until he was standing straight again, eyes once more hidden by the cowl.

'Begone, witch!' It came out in a deep, beastly growl, and a cold shudder ran through Megrin. He raised his head. Their eyes met and she recoiled as if she'd been struck.

'You are not Bodron,' she cried. 'Who are you? *What* are you?'

'I am your brother as ever was.' The voice came from the shadows, it echoed as if there was more than one speaker. 'And yet I am *more.*'

'Not . . . my . . . brother,' she repeated. Her voice sounded strangled and she felt her throat constrict as if an icy hand clamped on her neck. Cold oozed through her and as the pressure on her throat tightened, her vision began to blur and waver.

Megrin closed her eyes and fought back against the dark power, concentrating on the invisible stranglehold. She groaned with the effort, sagging to her knees. Then the pressure was gone, and she lurched forward, gasping for air.

'Begone,' the shadowed figure commanded.

For a second Megrin felt compelled to turn away, but she forced herself to resist. 'Not without the Copperplates.'

Bodron laughed again, an odd cacophony of voices overlapping one another.

'Take them,' he rumbled. 'If your power is equal to mine. And know this: I already have what you brought me.'

He raised the black staff and described a circle in the

air. Within it, a hazy image slowly came to focus.

Megrin saw Jack Flint painfully pull himself upright.

The heartstone dangled clearly from the open neck of his tunic.

Jack's head throbbed. His whole body felt like one big bruise. Carefully he sat up. For a moment looping vertigo made his vision blur and he closed his eyes tight until it went away.

Then the horrific memory of gargoyles and the creature with great leathery wings came back to him.

Jack shook the vision from his mind, not wanting to relive that moment or the mindless terror he had felt.

He tried to think back, to work out where he was. Corriwen and Kerry had been ahead of him, moving fast. He had run for the door, escaping the pull of that creature's will.

And then he had been falling, crashing down until everything faded. He looked groggily around, but there was no sign of his friends. He called for them, but heard only his voice reverberating around stone walls.

He forced himself to his feet, checking to ensure he still wore the heartstone, and that he still had the great sword and the leather satchel with the *Book of Ways* inside.

Then he took in his surroundings. He was on a wide spiral staircase. There was no banister of any sort, and each dusty wooden tread was fixed into a stone wall, without any other support. It felt flimsy and unsafe.

Looking up, he could see that the stairs spiralled for an impossible distance before disappearing into murk and dust. Vertigo made him sway again and he hugged the wall for support. He was trapped, confined and alone.

The steps below him took several turns before they reached a stone floor. It was darker down there, but logic told him he should take the lesser distance. Staying close to the wall, he descended carefully, until he reached the bottom and faced a blank, circular wall. A dead end.

In the centre of the floor there was a rusted metal grate with thick bars on what looked like the top of an ancient well, fastened by a single hoop. Jack approached it cautiously and peered down, expecting to see his reflection in the water. But there was nothing. The well seemed to go down as far as the stairway ascended.

Yet something was down there. The heartstone squeezed against him, just as a low vibration reverberated from the depths.

Jack drew back, fighting a curious compulsion to stay and see what was down there. He turned and scrambled up the steps, two at a time, feeling the stairs creak and dip alarmingly under his weight. When he thought he had gained enough height, he crawled to the edge of the steps and looked back down.

Something hit the metal grate with such force the heavy bars jumped upwards. They clanged back down again, and from behind them came a ferocious roar.

Jack recoiled, wondering if there was anywhere inside Bodron's domain that wasn't haunted by beasts and nightmares. Did Megrin's brother have monsters lying in wait at every turn? He couldn't answer that, but he knew he'd have to assume so, if he had any chance of staying alive here.

The creature in the well crashed again at the grate and Jack knew it was only a matter of time before the old metal gave way. He needed to get some more distance.

Jack continued up the stairway for another ten turns before stopping to look up, hoping to see a doorway or a landing. But there was nothing. Only the flimsy spiral steps going up and up until they disappeared in the distance.

Far below he heard the metal grate snap open and crash back against the floor. The trapped beast, now free, bellowed in triumph. Almost immediately came the hard thud of its weight on the treads. It sounded more like hooves than feet, but Jack didn't chance looking down. Ahead of him the staircase climbed impossibly high and he knew he couldn't keep running forever.

He recalled Megrin's warning: *Don't believe what you see, or what you hear.*

Think, he ordered himself, still not daring to pause on the stairs, because behind him he could hear the clatter of hooves on the treads growing ever louder. *Think!*

'Don't believe what you see or hear,' he repeated, speaking the words aloud. 'She means it's not real.'

Jack caught his breath and listened. The clatter of running hooves was closer now. He shouldered the satchel, grasped the hilt of the sword and started climbing again, as fast as he could, and then he forced himself to stop. Quickly he unhitched the satchel and drew out the *Book of*

Ways, placed it on a step, and tried to ignore the thudding approach from below.

The book opened and words began to scroll across the page.

As Jack bent to read, the letters squirmed and changed, a jumble of characters impossible to comprehend. He tried to focus on them, but it made his head ache. The letters spun and separated, crawling over the page like insects.

Desperately, he reached into his tunic and drew out the heartstone, cupped both hands around it, and looked again at the open book through the stone's smoky glass.

The lines on the page jumped into clarity and he read:

Journeyman finds all confusion
Caught in snare of bale illusion
Friend is lost in shadow land
Testing time is now at hand
Spellbind storm approaches swift
Heart will summon friend adrift.

He stared at the words, willing them to make sense. They always had before, even if the message was at first unclear. Below him, the beast on the stairs howled.

All confusion ... bale illusion ...

And Megrin's words were fresh and clear. *Don't believe.*

He closed his eyes, pressed the heartstone on his forehead, feeling its heat. He pictured himself, with Kerry and Corriwen together in sunlight on the lush grass of Uaine. The heart beat in time with his own pulse.

'I believe in my *friends*. I believe in the sword ... and in the *Book of Ways*!' His voice rose: 'I believe in the Sky Queen. I believe in the heartstone. All of them are real!'

He turned on the stair, eyes closed, but now shouting down the spiral.

'But I don't believe in *you*!'

The howl soared to a scream.

'*I . . . DON'T . . . BELIEVE!*'

A wave of pressure blasted up from below, rattling the flimsy steps, and a rumbling vibration shuddered the walls.

Jack pressed the heartstone tight against his skin.

'Corriwen,' he cried aloud. 'Kerry! Can you hear me?'

The stone wall beside him wavered like the surface of a pool. High overhead, the walls convulsed and a section of the stairway popped free and came tumbling towards him.

'Corriwen!'

The falling steps *whooshed* past as they fell and he hardly noticed them, for suddenly he could see Corriwen within the gleam of the heartstone, stumbling through a mist that came up to her chest. She cocked her head, as if she could hear him.

Jack concentrated hard. He thought he heard her voice, thin and muffled in the mist.

And behind that voice, he heard the sound of something that growled like a predator.

He saw Corriwen turn around wildly, trying to locate the sound Jack had heard.

'Run, Corrie. Run to me!' he shouted. 'To my voice!'

Under his feet, a powerful tremor shook the staircase and it began to disintegrate. The treads vibrated like springs and some of those higher up began to work themselves free. They dropped, one on top of another, like dominoes.

Jack raised his head and saw them plummet towards him in an avalanche of dusty wood. A noise like thunder swelled louder and louder as they slammed into lower ones and knocked them free, until all he could see was a mass of broken wood falling so fast it swept everything away.

And there was no way for him to escape.

SIXTEEN

Oh Bodron, what have you done?

Megrin fixed her eyes on him, standing motionless, while her mind searched along dark corridors and narrow passages, through halls and rooms until, at last, she found a place high in Bodron's Keep that her mind could not perceive. It was wreathed in a miasma of night.

This must where he kept the Copperplates, she thought. A secret place swathed in a hiding-spell.

She would have to find it, find the ancient Copperplates and then work out a way to reverse what Bodron had done.

And she had to find out what Bodron had done to Jack Flint, or what he planned for him. That plan, she knew, must involve the Journeyman's heartstone. Bodron meant to have it, and if he could corrupt its power as he had done with the Copperplates, who knew what might be unleashed?

'Begone, witch.' Bodron raised his staff and orange snakes of light coursed around it.

Without warning Megrin was slammed backwards by a force so powerful it felt as if all her bones would shatter. In a split second she managed to recover her wits and held her own staff upright.

Stop!

One word of command and all motion ceased.

The cowled figure stood stock still, before it turned and strode away from her. Blue fire licked around the carved head of her staff and she sent it towards him in a searing bolt. It wrapped itself around Bodron's receding form. He halted in mid-stride and she felt his enormous power fight against her. For a brief moment she was connected to the evil within him and felt utter revulsion. The strain of holding the binding-spell was so enormous she cried out. He turned to face her.

'You think your puny tricks can hold me?'

Under his hood, she saw a sly and hungry grin before he lowered his head and began to chant. 'Raging fire and bubbling stone ...'

Megrin heard those words clearly. Bodron stamped one foot and the chamber shook. Where his heel came down, a fissure opened in the stone floor, zig-zagging towards her. Yellow smoke hissed up and molten stone flowed across the floor, trapping her against the wall.

'River water, cool and clear.' Megrin sang aloud as she cast her own spell.

Her staff writhed in her hands. Bolts of blue light arced between its head and the stone wall and where they touched, cold water jetted from a dozen holes, cascading on to the molten rock in an eruption of sound and steam.

'Enough, Bodron,' Megrin cried. 'Give up what you have stolen from Uaine.'

He laughed a high cackle and spun on his heel.

The walls around her buckled and heaved. From holes in the stonework, misshapen things began to crawl out, yellow-eyed and scaled. Some spread leathery wings and took flight. Others crawled to the floor like spiders. Each of them a vision from hell.

Megrin quenched the fear that flared within her. These things were not real, yet within Bodron's domain, even the unreal could take shape and substance.

She shook the sleeves of her long coat. Two white cats landed on their feet beside her – her familiars, purring with anticipation.

The nightmares of Bodron's creation surged forward.

Megrin raised her staff. Her familiars leapt, their claws unsheathed. They met the onslaught in a flurry of motion, ripping and rending as the attacking horde hooked and stabbed, trying to reach Megrin.

Bodron turned away. His demonic laughter boomed over the screeching of the abominable creations as they were torn to pieces by the familiars and blasted from the air by the shafts from Megrin's staff.

She was too busy battling in the corner to stop him from leaving.

High above Jack, more steps cascaded down, dislodging the stones that held them in place. He forced himself flat against the wall despite the certainty that it could not shield him from the falling debris.

He bit back his fear and looked again at the heartstone. Through its crystal, he could see Corriwen running in the mist.

Behind her, Jack could also see a grey, powerful shape in pursuit. Its back was ridged with horny scales and its mouth opened to show rows of red teeth. He didn't know what it was. He didn't need to know.

'Run, Corriwen.' He cried. '*Run*!'

He saw her cock her head as if she'd heard his shout.

'Jack? *Jack?*' Her voice was muffled.

'Run, Corrie. *Run to my voice!*'

Jack could barely hear himself above the thunder of the collapsing stairway, but he knew Corriwen had heard him.

'Where are you, Jack?'

Behind her the beast snorted and wheeled around on thick legs. Jack saw scarlet eyes as it swung its head in Corriwen's direction, and accelerated its pace, heading directly for her.

'To my voice, Corrie. Come on!'

She didn't turn to look behind. She simply ran, clasping

her knives tightly on either side, her cape billowing behind her.

He could see her more clearly now, face pale, red hair whipped back, mouth agape as she gasped for breath.

The monster was getting closer, fifteen yards behind. Ten yards. Jack kept calling, to give her a direction.

She put on a last spurt of speed, racing directly towards Jack, while above him, ton after ton of splintering wood and crumbling masonry smashed into the stairs, nearly throwing him into the void.

Corriwen was yelling his name, her voice high and desperate.

Jack urged her on. He pressed himself hard against the cold stone wall.

Without warning, it gave under the pressure. His arms sank into it and he stumbled forward as the stone simply dissolved.

And suddenly Corriwen was there, yelling for him. Behind her the monster bunched ropy muscles, ready to pounce. Corriwen slammed into him with such force he was thrown backwards.

He felt them both pass through a filmy surface, and heard claws ripping at it with a horrendous tearing sound.

But they were out of the mist and back on the other side of the wall. An avalanche of timber and stone crashed down towards them as they tumbled over and over and over. Jack saw one massive block whirl in the air, cannon from wall to wall, expand in his vision as it bulleted towards them. He managed to twist, getting himself between the plummeting rock and Corriwen's fragile frame, even as he realised this would make no difference at all.

A huge weight clubbed him. He thought he heard his bones breaking, and a searing orange light exploded behind his eyes.

Then Jack and Corriwen were bouncing along on damp grass. When they finally stopped they lay there together, panting like hunted animals.

Jack groggily raised himself to his elbows, trying to get his eyes to focus. His head began to clear and he saw, a short distance away, the dim light of a candle glowing behind the window-pane in Megrin's woodland cottage.

SEVENTEEN

For a long while, all Jack could do was hold tight to Corriwen. She was trembling almost as much as he was in the aftermath. Somehow she was safe and they had both survived the collapse of the vast stairway.

'Are you okay?' he asked Corriwen finally.

'I don't know yet. But if you hadn't found me, I don't think I would be. I'd be, like Kerry would say, a goner?' She looked up at him. 'Where *is* Kerry?'

'I thought he was with you.'

Corriwen shook her head. 'No. I thought. Oh no! Is he still . . .?'

She didn't finish the sentence as the awful realisation hit them both. They had escaped from Bodron's Keep, but Kerry was still lost in that nightmare.

'How did we get out?' Corriwen was still confused.

'I've no idea. Megrin said there was a spell to keep people away. Maybe it spat us out.'

'We must get back there. We have to find Kerry.'

Jack nodded, although his heart sank at the thought of how long it might take to find their way to Bodron's Keep, and how long Kerry could survive within it.

'We need to think,' he said. He turned her around and she too noticed the cottage in the forest clearing.

'Look! It's Megrin's house.'

'I know,' Jack said. 'Back where we started. I've no idea how we got here, but we're a long way from Bodron's place.'

He looked around at the dark shadows in the forest. Overhead the moon was an angry red. 'Let's get inside. We shouldn't be out here at night.'

She grabbed his hand tightly and together they approached the wooden door.

It creaked slowly open as they stepped towards it. Corriwen started back, clutching Jack's arm. He peered cautiously inside, inhaling the aroma of warm food cooking on the open fire.

A movement beside the hearth caught his eye. Megrin's old chair was rocking back and forth. Jack drew Corriwen with him into the cottage.

'Who's there?' The rocking chair creaked and Megrin raised herself up, using her staff as a support.

She turned to look at them, and Corriwen gasped in alarm.

Megrin looked *old*, much older than she had when they had first met. Her hair, then silvery-grey, was now a tangle of white, and deep lines etched her face. Her staff was fire-blackened and badly splintered.

'Oh! Children. You made it out. Thank the stars. Thank the stars indeed.'

'What happened?' Jack asked, his thoughts in a whirl of confusion.

Megrin drew a hand wearily across her brow, and she swayed as though she were tired beyond exhaustion.

'It was you Bodron wanted. The Copperplates were bait for you and your heartstone.'

She lowered herself back into her seat. 'He knows its power and covets it. Like me, he knew you would come through the Faery Gate, and he waited a long time.'

'We don't know how we got back here,' Corriwen said.

'The heartstone protected you,' Megrin replied. Her skin was almost translucent, and her voice barely more than a whisper.

'He hunted you, through all his illusions. I tried to stop him, but I couldn't. He has grown too strong, with the power of the Copperplates. I fought him, and he almost finished me. There hasn't been a Geasan killed in Uaine for a thousand years and more, but he almost succeeded. His own sister too!'

'We've lost Kerry,' Corriwen blurted out. 'We have to go back for him.'

Jack looked around the little cottage. The table was set for three places, and once again he was reminded how like something out of a children's fairy tale it was.

'Kerry?' Megrin sounded confused, as if exhaustion had clouded her memory. 'Oh, yes. Is he not with you?'

'We were in a big hall. There were awful things in there and we ran. I saw him running out the door. Then I lost him.'

Megrin sighed. 'He's not here. I don't know where he might be. Bodron cast a *geas* on me and I found myself back here, as if I had never even been in that dark place.'

She ran a gaunt hand down her face. 'But I know I have been there. The pain of it still wracks me.'

Corriwen moved towards her and wrapped her arms around the old woman. She felt so thin and weak it seemed her bones might break. Corriwen shuddered at the touch of the old woman's wasted frame and pulled away quickly.

'So . . . drained,' Megrin whispered. 'Thank you, my dear, for sharing your warmth and your strength. At least you are safe here.'

'But Kerry isn't,' Jack said urgently. 'We have to go back for him.'

The old woman shook her head. 'I fear he may be lost. Bodron's power is too great.'

'No!' Corriwen gasped, her face pale. 'Not Kerry. He can't be.'

Megrin's eyes met Jack's with an expression of deep sorrow and regret. His heart felt suddenly leaden. The thought of Kerry – he couldn't even bring himself to say that word – was just too much to bear.

'Sit,' Megrin said kindly. 'Come and eat. Save your strength.'

She ushered Corriwen to the table. Jack followed, numb with worry. Megrin sat at the end, in front of the third plate and spooned some stew out into wooden bowls.

The heartstone pulsed hard on his chest.

Something is wrong, he thought. Something's *badly* wrong.

He tried to reassure himself. Perhaps it was the shock of realising they had escaped from the nightmare and Kerry was still trapped within it, still running from beasts and monsters. Maybe they had caught him. Maybe ... all of this was tumbling through Jack's mind in a confusing and frightening maelstrom.

'Eat, Jack Flint. Before it gets cold.'

Jack looked down at the bowl, filled to the brim with stew and vegetables. It should have been appealing and it seemed a long time since he had last eaten, but Jack had no appetite. Corriwen fidgeted on her stool, pale in the firelight, unable to stay still. He could tell she wanted to move, to fight. To do *something*.

'Eat up, girl,' Megrin urged.

On the table, a basket was filled to the brim with scones still warm from the oven and golden-crusted loaves of bread.

Something's wrong here, Jack's inner voice insisted, although he couldn't work out what. The heartstone was still beating fast. Corriwen's eyes met his across the table. They were full of questions, but Jack's mind was reeling with his fear for Kerry and the sensation of something badly amiss. He couldn't get his thoughts in order.

'You really should eat the food,' Megrin said. Her voice had a rough edge, as if she had a cold coming on. 'And rest the night here, where it's safe.'

'How can I eat?' he said. 'Kerry's still in there!' He

pushed the stool back and crossed to the little window.

'Where are you going? Come back to the table.' Megrin croaked the words now. 'Get back and eat the food I spent so long baking and cooking for you.'

Three plates. The thought struck him as even more odd than Megrin's suddenly querulous tone of voice. He looked through the window.

What he saw made him gasp in horror. It was the great hall from Bodron's Keep. Grotesque imps caroused around the table, tearing at whatever came to hand, stuffing it into their mouths in disgusting handfuls.

And in the tall chair, with its back to him, a dark and huddled shape began to turn towards him once again. Jack felt as if he'd been speared with ice.

'Oh!' He couldn't manage anything else and spun away.

'I told you to get back,' Megrin snapped. Her voice was rough as sand.

Illusion, Jack told himself. Just a picture. They were safe here in Megrin's cottage. Or was this an illusion too?

The hairs on his neck were standing on end. Corriwen's eyes sought his and he saw they were wide with alarm.

'What's wrong with you, boy? Have you no respect at all?' Megrin's hand found his shoulder and her fingers tightened hard, digging in at his collarbone with such strength that Jack winced.

He squirmed away and saw something glitter in her tar-black eyes. She grinned, displaying a row of long yellow-stained teeth. Jack's heart leapt to his throat.

Corriwen cried out suddenly and jerked back from the table.

From her bowl, fat maggots were crawling their way over the rim, twitching.

'What's happening?' One of the maggots slipped onto the surface and burst open. A green liquid spilled out, hissing as it ate into the wood.

Jack backed away. Corriwen's hands were shaking.

'Eat,' Megrin snarled. 'Eat the damned food, you ungrateful wretches.'

Her voice had strengthened. It was as deep and hoarse as a man's.

They turned to face her. Corriwen gasped.

Megrin was standing, both hands on the table. Knotted, calloused hands covered in black hairs. Her nails were long and horny and her face was bloated and studded with dark blisters.

But her eyes! Her eyes were black as coals and empty as space.

Jack recoiled from them. *It's not Megrin!* his mind jabbered. Whatever it was, it had lured them into a trap. He felt a sudden rush of fury.

Instinctively, Jack pushed Corriwen behind him while the thing that was not Megrin began to laugh, deep and rasping. The blisters on its face cracked and split. Its skin peeled away and any resemblance to Megrin Willow was gone.

A tall, bearded man wreathed in a smoky shadow stood in front of them. The image flickered and wavered, merging from one form to another, until all Jack could see was a dark shape that sucked the light from the room. From it emanated a powerful sensation of hate and anger.

It wrapped around Jack in a cloak of such utter foulness he thought he might never break free of it.

'Jack!' He heard Corriwen's voice, far off. He hardly felt her tugging at his hood as a long arm stretched towards him, reaching for the heartstone on his chest.

There was nothing he could do to stop it.

EIGHTEEN

'What do you mean you never had a friend?'

Kerry was lying comfortably, his weight on one elbow, on the bank of the stream. The girl with gold-flecked eyes sat elfin-like opposite him, her face cupped in both hands, studying him with great intensity.

At first he thought he must be dead and that she must be an angel.

The last thing he could remember was running in the tunnel and the water slamming him in the back. The next instant he was lying on warm grass. All around him, the sweet scent of flowers filled the air. Somewhere close, a little stream burbled over pebbles. Birds sang clear in musical notes.

And then he'd seen the girl, a slight figure sitting on a smooth stone, bare feet at the edge of the water. She had hair the colour of summer corn and wide, lustrous brown eyes.

'Hello!' It was all he could think to say.

She stared at him silently.

'Are you an angel?' Kerry began. She shook her head.

'A fairy? Something like that?'

He was totally confused. How had he suddenly arrived here? Wherever *here* was.

The girl smiled and her eyes sparkled.

'I am Rionna. This is *my* place.'

'Hi, Rionna. I'm Kerry. At least, I *was* Kerry. I don't know what I am now. Is this like heaven? Or limbo?'

'It's my place,' she said, still smiling. 'I brought you here.'

She walked across the shallow water towards him, making neither sound nor splash, and knelt in front of him.

'You were in danger,' she said. 'I felt your fear. It called to me. Here there is no fear.'

Tentatively she reached out a delicate hand and touched his.

'Welcome, Kerry. Safe in Rionna's haven.'

'I don't know how you did it, but thanks. I can't swim.'

She leant closer, examining his face. Her free hand touched him on the side of his nose.

'What are these things? These marks?'

At first he was taken aback and touched his skin where she did. Their fingers met and a strange jolt sent a shiver up his arm.

'Oh, these? They're freckles. I get them all the time,

being Irish. You want to see me in summer. I'm like a freakin' leopard.'

She held his hand, her fingers warm.

'I knew someone would come, one day. I am glad it's you. I never saw a Kerry before.'

'Oh, no. I'm just a boy.'

She frowned, puzzled. 'A boy?'

'Yes. Just a kid. Well, a bit more than a kid.' He grinned. 'You mean to say you never met a boy before?'

She shook her head. 'I never met *anyone* before.'

'Well, just wait until you meet my friends.'

Rionna leaned closer until they were almost nose to nose. She smelt of apple-blossom.

'What is a *friend*?'

'What? You mean you never had a friend?' Kerry asked incredulously. 'Everybody's got friends. I've got Jack and Corriwen. Best friends I ever had.'

'Where are they?'

'I dunno. We were in this room and I . . . I . . . *saw* things. I just grabbed Corrie and pushed her out. I've been scared before, but this was different. It was like every bad thing in the world was going to happen. If I hadn't run, I think I'd have dropped dead on the spot.'

He lowered his head in shame. 'But Corrie wasn't outside and I fell down a hole. And Jack, well I don't know what's happened. I shouldn't have left them, but I couldn't help it.'

'*It* makes fear,' she said. 'It makes terror and it feeds on it.'

'What does? The thing in the chair? That was a Roak. A

big carrion bird from Temair. But this wasn't like any Roak I've seen before, believe me. It was the worst thing ever, times ten. It reached right into me, honestly it did.'

'It only shows what it wants you to see,' Rionna said. 'It's a soul-eater. That's why I sang this haven. It's where I come to be free of it, out from its shadow.'

Kerry sat up, now even more confused. 'I don't think I got any of that. You mean you live in there? In that nightmare castle? And you *sang* this place?'

'I made a song in my heart,' she said. 'I sang *here* into being. Here is peace and safety. Beyond is madness. I have watched it grow strong and dark, and I have hidden from it for a long time.'

'Wow! If you can sing a place like this into existence, you'd be a smash hit at karaoke. That's a fine talent you've got.'

'I heard you. It sowed the nightmare in your heart and your heart cried out to me. I urged you on and you came.'

'That was you?' He recalled the sing-song in his head. *Water comes, water goes, water rises, water flows . . .* 'I thought I'd flipped my lid.'

She looked at him, uncomprehending. Kerry grinned. 'Gone loony. Pure mental.' He made a clockwise sign with his finger at his temple, but she didn't seem to have a clue what he meant.

'What about Jack and Corrie? What happened to them? '

She shook her head. 'I don't know. I only heard you. You were in tune. You must have a good heart.'

Kerry blushed. 'No. That's Jack Flint you're thinking

about. He's the good guy. The Journeyman.'

She smiled at him. 'Maybe, but your heart is true, and it called to me. That's why I opened a way.'

He gave her his hand and she clasped it.

'I appreciate it, I really do. Another step and I'd have been a goner. An ex-Kerry.'

She laughed, clear and innocent. Kerry got the impression she didn't do that too often.

'It's a lovely place you got here. Look at the size of those trout! One of them would feed a family.'

She laughed again and turned to look into the water. He saw her lips move and one of the big fish peeled away from the far bank and swam to the shallows, then gave a little flip and beached itself on the shingle.

'For you,' she said.

He shook his head and nudged the trout back.

'That one looked tasty for sure, but it wouldn't be sporting, would it? Now, if I could do that back home, I'd have no need of hooks and lines.'

'What is this *home*?'

'Oh, that's where I come from. Me and Jack, we live in Scotland, but there's this ring of standing stones, and when you go through . . .'

And once he'd started, he found he couldn't stop telling her of how they'd stumbled between the standing stones to land in Temair, how they had found Corriwen. He told her all of their adventures while she listened, fascinated.

'A great hero you must be, Kerry,' Rionna said when he'd finished. 'And to have such friends. I knew you had a good heart.'

‘I can’t believe I left them. To tell the truth, I was scared rigid. After I saw that thing, I was right out the door. Next second, I was in a tunnel with all that water at my back.’

Kerry sat up to face her again. ‘What exactly is this thing?’

‘Something brought from the underworlds to Uaine. I remember sunshine and stars when I was young, but they are long gone. This brought the darkness.’

‘But what is it? We were told it’s got something to do with Copperplates, which I don’t know much about. They were stolen by some magician guy called Bodron.’

Rionna lowered her head and closed her eyes for a second. To Kerry it felt as if a cloud had passed in front of the sun.

When she started to speak, Kerry sat still and listened.

‘Bodron is ... *was* ... my father,’ Rionna began. ‘I barely remember him now, as he was, before he opened the Dark Way.

‘And then everything changed.

‘I remember my mother. She was beautiful; golden hair and shining eyes. She died when I was very little.

‘I didn’t know it then, but I know now, that he cast a binding on her so that she lay still and never changed, and he beseeched the Sky Queen to bring her back, but she never answered.

‘And from his despair came anger, dark anger. I was a baby, but I could sense his rage and was afraid of it. An old woman nursed me then, and but for her, I might have starved.

‘My father travelled to far places, and when he returned

he was very different. Something burned in his soul. He brought us to this old keep to begin his work.

'That is when the darkness came.'

Rionna paused. Her eyes were wide, but Kerry could see they were focused far in the past. He sat quietly and waited for her to continue.

'By the time I had learned to walk, I found a way to travel *between* places. Perhaps a gift from my mother, who was a Geasan woman from a far world beyond the standing gates. And it is just as well. Because what came with the darkness was cold as death, and hungry too. The keep became a place of shadows and strange things.

'I could wander unseen and slip between, to where I wanted to go. I would sit with my mother in the secret place where she lay, pale as a cloud, and hope that perhaps she might draw a breath and free my father from his bane. But she never did.

'From my hidden place, I watched him work night after day, consulting the shining pages he had sought in far-off places, until one day he found a way to put them in order.

'I remember the change in the air at that moment. The dead coals in the hearth burst into orange flame, though the air turned cold, and in the middle of his chamber appeared a dark pit that led to who knows where. From it, something looked out, something that defied the eye, hurt the soul.

'I had read his scripts, and I knew that this was a beast of dark places summoned to Uaine. And it brought its own minions – the nightshades.

'From that day I lived in fear and hid in the between

places until I learned to make this haven with my song. Not even that demon can find me here.'

'But why did your father want to conjure up a creepy monster?'

'Because he thought the Sky Queen had abandoned him. He summoned a lord of darkness and promised it Uaine if it would bring my mother back to life.'

'And did it work?'

She shook her head. 'What soul has gone to Tir-nan-Og may never return. She moved, the way a statue might move, but never talked. If this was life, then it wasn't how we would think of it. Whatever came from that pit was in her, and her shape stalked the halls and passageways at night when the moon turned to blood.

'It searched for me with a hunger I could feel in my soul, and from that day I have hidden.'

'Just as well,' Kerry said.

'A long time to be alone,' Rionna said, 'but here in my song-place, I have peace. While in my father's world, the beast waits.'

'For what?' Kerry asked, bemused.

'For the talisman. I would listen to my father talk to himself. The demon has promised him that the empty thing that walks the shadows will be given true life when it has the Heart of Worlds in its possession.

'The heart?' Kerry sat up quickly. He only knew of one heart, the one Jack wore round his neck.

'Yes. The key to worlds. An ancient power that will allow the beast to bind Uaine to its black place and build a gateway for its legions. There are two hearts, each pure, created by the Sky Queen long ago. It already has one of them. When it has its twin, the gates of the underworlds will be thrown open. After that, madness and terror.'

'It's Jack's heart!' Kerry couldn't stop himself. 'The Key to Worlds. It's the Journeyman's heart.'

'You know of it?'

'Know of it. Jeez, I've seen it. I've *held* it. The Morrigan nearly killed me for it. Jack got it from his father.'

'And it is here in Uaine?'

'It's in your father's castle. 'Cos that's where Jack is, him and Corrie Redthorn.'

Rionna's eyes went wide with alarm. 'Then he is in awful danger, Kerry. I know from my father's scripts that he almost had both hearts in his possession, many years ago, and would have had it but for the courage of the bearer, who fought the shades and escaped.'

'That must have been Jack's dad. Jack was just a baby at the time.'

'It will not fail this time. It has waited a long time, as my father has weakened and wasted until I see nothing of him at all, just the dark hunger he has raised from the pit.'

Kerry got to his feet, and helped Rionna up. The sun was warm on his back and the scent of flowers filled the clean air. He would have given anything to stay a while in Rionna's secret world. *Almost* anything.

'Listen, Rionna. I'd love to hang about here, but I have to find Jack. I left him in that hall, with those ... those things. He'd never do that to me.'

Kerry felt tears sting his eyes and blinked them back. 'I'm so ashamed. So I *have* to find him, no matter what.'

'There is only danger where he is.'

'I've done danger before.' He raised his face and pugnaciously stuck out his chin. 'I've nearly been a goner too many times to count, but you can't keep an Irish fella down. Jack's my friend. The best you could ask for. I have to get back and help him.'

Rionna smiled up at him, slender and elfin, and her eyes sparkled in the sunlight.

'I *knew* you were a hero, Kerry the traveller. I have waited so long to meet a friend.'

She took him by the hand and led him alongside the brook. A short distance downstream, she stopped at a place where a smooth rock overhung a deep pool. Holding tight to his hand, she raised her own over the water and Kerry heard a pure sound, like the crystal clear song of the golden harp on Tara Hill. She motioned him to look down.

The water swirled, and far down below the surface, an image began to take shape.

In the depths, he saw Jack Flint and Corriwen Redthorn approach Megrin's forest cottage.

A shadow passed over the water and when it cleared he saw them again, though now they were standing by a table, clutching each other. For an instant he was so surprised that he didn't recognise the place, but he recognised the look of horror on their faces.

On the very edge of the scene, he saw Megrin reaching out towards them as the skin of her face peeled away in papery strips. Underneath it was something as dark as night.

Jack's heartstone glinted as a long tendril reached from the dark, forming a claw-like hand.

Kerry jumped to his feet. Rionna's song cut off instantly.

'It's not where you think,' Rionna said.

'I have to help them. How do I get out of here?'

She looked at him, her eyes glowing.

'There is terrible danger. I saw the heartstone. The demon has seen it too and covets it, and I fear for all of Uaine if it succeeds.'

'Well, I've got to stop that thing,' Kerry cried. 'And to hell with the danger. That's my friends it's messing with.'

She nodded and motioned to him to look down. She began her song again, making small gestures with her free hand. The surface of the water rippled, followed the direction of her delicate fingers until it looked like a miniature version of a great whirlpool.

Kerry looked down into a galaxy of glittering stars slowly revolving in the depths. In the centre of them all, he saw the familiar crown of five bright stars,

'The Corona,' he whispered. 'The Sky Queen's crown.'

Starlight sent beams of luminescence up from the surface until Kerry and Rionna were bathed in the light.

Rionna reached out, and the light wove around her fingers in strings of energy which she gathered together and wound until her hands blazed. It was as if she had harvested the light of a thousand winking stars and gathered it to herself.

'Come, Kerry,' she said softly. She lowered the pulsing light almost to the surface, and one by one, the reeds at the water's edge curled around it, weaving themselves into a basket that encased the light.

Rionna led him back to the rock overlooking the water and began to sing softly.

Kerry looked down again and saw Jack Flint shrink back from the reaching claw, one hand scrabbling for the great sword on his belt and the other moving to cover the heartstone. Corriwen was pushing past him, slashing with her glittering knife in a slow-motion dance.

'You wish to face this?' Rionna asked, and Kerry sensed the question in his head, for her crystal song still filled the air.

'I have to,' Kerry replied. His throat was dry and made his voice croak.

'I knew you had a good heart,' Rionna said. Without pause, she tugged at his hand. Kerry was taken by surprise as he felt his weight tip forward and then he was falling.

'I can't swim,' he blurted, as the surface came up to meet him.

Together they plunged into the pool.

Kerry gasped for air. None would come. He felt himself tumble into icy cold. Rionna's fingers were still clamped tightly to his wrist. His lungs hitched as he searched for breath.

Then they were not in water. They were flying, tumbling down through circles of luminescence. Rionna turned to him and smiled. Her free hand reached out and stroked his cheek as if to soothe his fears.

As her fingers touched him, Kerry landed hard on his feet, with such force he was driven to his knees and a shock of impact jolted through his bones. His ears popped and air flooded his lungs. Warm, smoky air, maybe, but air. He knelt on solid ground, whooping like an exhausted runner.

'Quick,' Rionna urged. 'We must move. No time to waste.'

She snatched his arm and they raced down a dark passage very like the one where he had heard the bestial grunt in the dark.

'Where are we? This isn't Megrin's house.'

'That was an enchantment. Nothing is real in this place. But what's not real can still harm.'

'You're worse than the *Book of Ways*,' Kerry said. 'All riddles.'

They came to an old door and Rionna pushed it open.

'Jack!'

Kerry appeared by his shoulder. Jack saw him stumble forward, almost into the creature's reach.

A small figure pushed past him, lithe as a cat. Jack glimpsed a pale face and wide eyes. A girl.

She tore at something in her hands. Pieces of green reed shredded in her fingers and then light exploded, so blinding and fierce that everything stood out in black and white. The heartstone seemed to suck the light into itself. Jack felt its heat on his chest.

The twisting shape hissed like a snake, but the pause

gave Jack the time he needed to draw his sword. He swung it as the claw snatched for the stone again and he felt the blade shudder as it pierced the mass of shadow. An ear-splitting shriek ruptured the air.

The light in the girl's cupped hands arced between the sword and the heartstone and the dark shape shrank back into itself. The shriek rose to a hurricane roar as shards of light stabbed out from the sword blade.

Jack held his sword steady, his face lit up by the girl's magical light.

Then the creature was gone. Nothing remained but smoke and a reek of sulphur on the air.

Jack slowly lowered his sword and sank to his knees.

There was a long silence before anyone spoke. Finally it was Kerry who did.

'Another fine mess we had to get you out of.'

NINETEEN

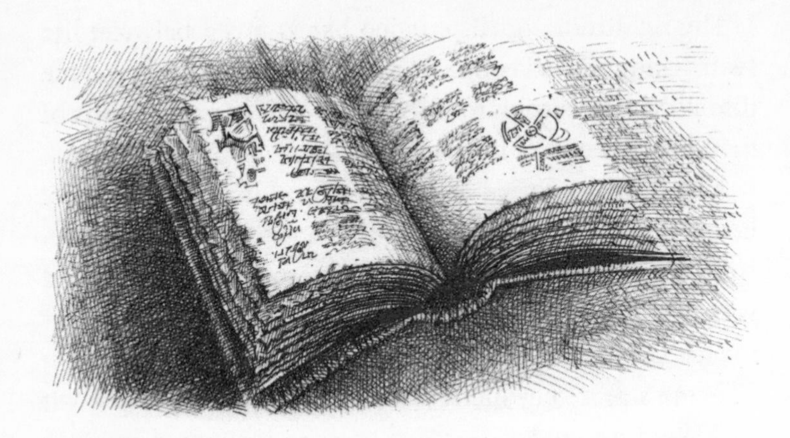

Megrin wiped her brow on her sleeve, resting for a moment whilst the remaining apparitions crumbled to dust. Whether they had been real, or simply illusions, even Megrin could not tell. But she knew that whatever they were, they had served only as a distraction to keep her here; to separate her from Jack Flint and the heartstone talisman that he carried.

The boy was her main concern. Jack Flint was vitally important because of what he carried. The Journeyman's heartstone.

Megrin closed her eyes and allowed her senses to reach out. In her mind she kept the image of the deep and secret chamber she'd seen before, hidden in wreaths of enchantment that proved too strong a barrier to her own powers.

That, she was sure, was where she would find the power that brought the shadows to Uaine. The power that was now using her brother's form for its own malevolent purpose.

Megrin strode forward, using her staff for balance, her feet kicking up little puffs of dust, the last remnants of the devils that had been summoned to hold her. She reached the place where the foot of the staircase had been.

There was nothing here now. Even Bodron's guttural laugh could no longer be heard.

Her mind was unable to locate Jack and his friends, which meant one of two things. Either they were no longer inside Bodron's Keep, or they were, but they had been taken to a place beyond her reach.

Beyond an arched doorway, a corridor forked left and right. She chose the left hand path. It descended into shadows and Megrin felt her heart trip faster as she walked down.

The sword slipped from Jack's fingers and sent up sparks when it clanged on the flagstones.

'Kerry!' Jack cried.

He leapt up and grabbed Kerry by the front of his tunic, bunching the material in his fists as he dragged him forward. His face was red and his voice tight with emotion as he shook him back and forth.

'Where the *hell* have you been?'

Kerry's jaw dropped in amazement. But before he could say a word, Jack pulled him close, threw his arms around him and squeezed him in such a bear hug he felt his ears pop.

'Jeez, man,' Jack said, right in his ear. 'We thought you were a goner!' Relief surged through Jack. The thought of losing Kerry, his best friend since childhood, had defied description.

'I very nearly was, believe me,' Kerry began. But now Corriwen had her arms around his neck and squeezed him even tighter. Tears ran unashamedly down her cheeks.

'Hang on, hang on. Let me breathe.' Kerry tried to pull back, laughing and gasping at the same time. Jack loosened his grip and released him. Even in the dark, he could see Kerry was blushing deep red.

'How did you get here?' Jack wanted to know. 'And who's the girl?'

'And where is *here*?' Corriwen added. She looked around at walls hung with shredded tapestries. 'We were in Megrin's place and she ... she changed into ...'

'I know. We saw you. Me and Rionna. We came to help.'

'You and who?'

Kerry turned. Rionna had backed into a corner where she was hidden in shadows.

'Rionna, come and meet Jack and Corrie.' He reached for her and gently drew her forward into the light.

Jack stared at Rionna. This elfin girl had come between him and the shadowed monster, blinding it with light. She had given him his chance.

'Rionna, this is Jack Flint and Corriwen Redthorn. My

best friends. Guys, this is Rionna, and if it wasn't for her, you'd be mincemeat by now. Me too. She knew what to do. She's brilliant.'

'Slow down,' Jack said. 'Back up. Who is she? Where's she from?'

Kerry was too excited to stop. 'We jumped into the water and we came to help you.'

'Kerry Malone jumped in water? Not in a million years.'

'Well, Rionna pulled me, actually. But honest, that's how we got here. Rionna's got this place. It's magic. Really beautiful.' He put an arm round her shoulder and drew her closer. 'Isn't that right?'

The girl nodded slowly.

'But who is she?' Corriwen asked. 'And how did you find her?'

'She's Bodron's daughter.'

'*Bodron*'s daughter?' Jack shrank back, his mind running into overdrive. Was this another trick? Another illusion? Would she suddenly change into something *else*? His hand reached automatically for his sword and fumbled with the empty scabbard.

The girl's face slackened in dismay.

'How could you bring her? Look at everything he's done. You don't even know if she's real! She could be a trick, just like Megrin was.'

Rionna tried to shrink back into the shadows again, but Kerry held her wrist.

'She's real all right,' Kerry retorted. 'And don't forget, she's just saved your hide. And mine too. You should be grateful, so you should.'

'But *Bodron*'s daughter ...' Jack looked from Kerry to the girl. He couldn't understand how Kerry could have been so stupid as to bring the enemy into their midst. He had trusted people before and been wrong. Jack's head was still spinning from the horror of what had happened in Megrin's cottage and now the shock of finding themselves back in Bodron's Keep.

'So what if she is his daughter?' Kerry snorted. 'Megrin's her aunt, isn't she? And look at me. My dad's in jail, but that doesn't make me a crook, does it?'

Before Jack could reply, Kerry went charging on.

'No buts, Jack. Not this time.' He put his arm around Rionna's shoulders again, and held her protectively. 'She's with me. With *us*. We got a new friend. If it wasn't for her, I wouldn't be here. And neither would you.'

Kerry's free hand was bunched, as if he was ready to fight. 'She brought the corona-light with her. That's what chased the monster away. She saved all of us.'

The girl found her voice. It was soft, but very clear, almost musical.

'Bodron was my father. But he brought something into this world that infested him, sucked out the man that he was. That is what you should fear, for I have feared it all my life. I will help you, because Kerry asks.'

She drew back behind Kerry again. Corriwen stepped forward.

'Forgive us, Rionna, Bodron's daughter,' she said. She took the girl's hands and raised them to her own cheeks.

'If you saved Kerry, then we are in your debt. And you

helped us when we needed it most. The Redthorn always repay.'

Rionna smiled shyly.

Kerry stared meaningfully at Jack, whose hand was on the heartstone, hiding it from view. Jack finally nodded and took his hand away. The heartstone gleamed with its own deep life.

'I'm sorry, Kerry,' Jack finally spoke. 'For what I said. And to you, Rionna. My head's all screwed up and confused.'

'Confused?' Kerry interrupted. 'I was scared to death. But she's the real McCoy, is Rionna. Wait till you see her place. Man, the size of the fish! And fruit that tastes like nothing on earth.'

Jack picked up his sword and sheathed it. Kerry was right. The girl was not responsible for what her father had done, and now she too was an orphan as much as Corriwen Redthorn. He placed his hand on Rionna's. Her fingers trembled.

'Rionna. I'm very sorry for what I said. Any friend of Kerry's is a friend of ours. I don't know what you did or how you did it, but I'm awfully glad you did.'

She looked into his eyes.

'You are Jack, the Journeyman. The heartstone-holder.' She held his hand surprisingly tightly. 'Come to save Uaine.'

'I don't know if I can. Or if anybody can.'

'If you cannot, then no one can. I see into your heart, and it is true.'

This time it was Jack's turn to blush to his roots.

Kerry stepped forward. 'Okay, Jack. Enough of the smooth talk. You can't steal all the girls.'

And suddenly the three friends burst into gales of laughter, releasing the tension. Rionna stared at them as if they had gone mad.

The laughter took a while to subside, and despite the circumstances, they felt strengthened by it. It was the one natural thing in this unnatural place.

They found a small chamber where Kerry managed to light the wick of an old oil lamp. The feeble light made their faces glow in the gloom.

'So what next?' Kerry spoke, but all eyes were on Jack.

'We have two choices. Get the hell out of here – if we can even find a way out – or stay and find these Copperplates. They're the answer.'

'That's no choice, Jack Flint, and you know it,' Corriwen snorted. 'You didn't venture alone through the Faery Gate just to run away.'

'No. I didn't,' Jack replied.

'But it's not just the Copperplates,' Kerry butted in. 'It's the heartstone too. That's what Bodron wants. There's two of them, and he's already got one of them. Rionna told me.'

Jack turned to Rionna. 'Two heartstones? What's this about?'

'There are two heartstones,' Rionna explained. 'They are the keys to all worlds. My father used the Copperplates to unlock the Dark Way, but with the heartstones he can throw the gates open and let the demons from below into Uaine.'

'Why would he want to do that?'

'Because he is no longer my father. What came through the nether-gate is now inside him. It works its will through him.'

'So what next?' Kerry repeated.

'I think it's going to get really dangerous.'

'We know that, Jack,' Kerry retorted. 'We knew it on Temair and in Eirinn. We're with you no matter what. What's the difference here?'

'The difference is that I don't know how to fight this,' Jack said. He was supposed to be the one with the answers, but all he had were questions. 'In Temair and in Eirinn, we knew what we were up against. We could *see* them. But how do you fight illusions? We don't even know where we are or where we have to go.'

'You could ask the *Book of Ways,*' Corriwen suggested. 'It might tell us.'

'I hope so, because I'm all out of ideas at the moment. We thought everything was okay until Megrin started to change into something ...'

'It wasn't Megrin,' Corriwen said.

'It was a demon,' Rionna agreed. 'Something conjured up from the Underplace.'

'If we go on,' Jack continued, 'and if we do find Megrin, then we will have to face Bodron. And finish him.'

'I think it would be better for him to be free of it,' Rionna said. Her face was filled with sad acceptance. 'One way or another.'

'Consult the book,' Corriwen insisted again.

Jack sat down and the others joined him. He set the *Book of Ways* on the floor in front of them. It opened and the pages whirred in succession as if stirred by a wind, then stopped.

They waited, but the page remained blank.

'Maybe the battery died,' Kerry said, trying lighten the mood.

A crimson blot appeared on the top of the page.

'What . . .?' Jack smelled the coppery scent of blood. As he fixed his eyes on the thick blot, it welled even thicker.

'Blood,' Corriwen hissed. Kerry was looking up, trying to see where it had come from, but there was no stain on the arched ceiling.

Jack concentrated on the page. The blot became a trickle, sluggishly moving across the page and then a line of it streaked diagonally downwards, as if drawn by a sharp nail. Jack jerked back.

Another line slashed two semi-circles on the first. It was a capital B. And without pause the invisible nail scrawled one word.

BLOOD

Then it began to scrawl faster and faster until the page was filled with bloody words in jagged letters.

Blood to drink and flesh to rend
Children suffer 'til the end
Feast on terror, feast on fright
Feast on eyes bereft of sight
Too late to flee, too late to run
The dying time has now begun
Mortal souls forever lost
The hour has come to pay the cost

'Jeez . . .' Kerry muttered.

'The writing's all different,' Jack said aghast. 'This can't be right. It's always warned us before, but that's a threat!'

And as he spoke the line of blood zig-zagged in a series of jolting lines beneath which a new line of words appeared like knife-slashed wounds:

You are NOW MINE!

The *Book of Ways* shuddered. Acrid fumes rose up from the violent lines of verse, and two tongues of flame appeared. The page began to burn through.

The book bucked. Its leather covers flapped up and down. Before Jack could move, it snapped shut with the force of a hammer-blow.

For a moment all went still, but it was not over. The cover slowly creaked open. Jack held his breath as the pages whirred once more. He expected to see a charred ruin, but instead when the pages stopped, he saw only some fine ash blow off the page like dust, leaving a clean blank leaf. He could see no other damage at all.

Now, new words began to appear on the pages, and this time they were written in the old familiar script.

Follow terror, follow fright
Walk beyond the darkest night
Fear behind, fear before
On until the final door
Madness there holds evil sway
Horror waits for mortal prey
Find the hidden secret room
Journeyman must face his doom

Jack looked up. His face was sickly pale.

'That's the real message,' he said shakily. 'The other one … that was from whatever is doing all this. It's playing games with us.'

'The second message is bad enough,' Kerry said.

For a long time, nobody spoke. Jack closed his eyes and rubbed them slowly, as if he was very tired.

'Well, we know where to go,' he finally said.

'I don't understand,' Corriwen whispered.

'We just keep walking. The worse it gets, the closer we'll be.'

Kerry put his hand on his friend's shoulder and gripped tight.

'All for one,' he said. 'We're still with you.'

TWENTY

For hours Megrin stumbled through passages and tunnels, and as she descended, the hot smell of sulphur mixed with the dank reek of decay, in a foul mixture that would have made a lesser mortal choke.

It was closer now, wreathed in shadows. Not Bodron. It was something from the shadowed underworld, something that had come through the Dark Way. It was powerful and devoid of any human quality.

She walked carefully on, sensing her way towards the source when she felt a sudden shudder under her feet and in the fabric of the thick air. The jolt sent seismic tremors through the ground and she knew that something had happened.

She stopped in the gloom and slowed her breath. And then she felt it.

Jack Flint and his friends were here. They were far away, Jack and Kerry and Corriwen Redthorn, and still inside Bodron's black reach. While her heart lurched at the thought of them in danger, a part of her surged in the knowledge that they were still alive.

It meant that the heartstone's bearer was still pursuing his quest, as she had foreseen. His friends would be behind him every step of the way, no matter where it led.

It was the bravery and determination in the hearts of these three young people, that she had long known would be the only salvation for Uaine.

Megrin walked on towards what awaited her in the deep tunnels under Bodron's Keep.

She wanted to face Bodron before Jack Flint did, because she knew he needed the heartstone to complete his plans.

And that could mean only one thing. The final opening of the Dark Way between Uaine and the shadowlands below.

It could mean the end of everything.

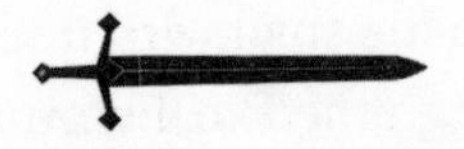

'The worse it gets, the closer we'll be,' Jack repeated, as they walked along the narrow tunnel.

It had been bad already, and none of them knew how bad it could get. But his friends were with him and that lent Jack courage.

'Which way then?' Kerry asked, when they reached a place where several passageways intersected. Jack didn't reply for a moment, then he turned slowly from left to right, in almost a full circle. He stopped and pointed to the left.

'That way,' he said.

'How do you know?' Rionna's voice was a whisper in the gloom.

'I don't know how. I think the heartstone knows where danger lies.'

'I'm scared already,' Kerry admitted. His short-sword was out, but he had a fair idea it wouldn't be much good against nightmares.

He'd much rather be on the banks of Rionna's stream, catching trout with his bare hands and soaking up the sun. In fact, he told himself, he'd rather be anywhere at all.

'Might as well get it over with,' he added, even though his heart was pounding. 'Just as long as I don't meet the monster with claws from under my bed, I'll be fine.'

He walked behind the others, guarding their backs, with Rionna ahead and Corriwen close on Jack's heels. There wasn't room to walk side by side.

The tunnel sloped down in a spiral, and as they descended, the air seemed to become thicker. Corriwen held the little oil-lamp at shoulder height and the tiny flame allowed Jack to see a couple of feet ahead, but no more.

The heartstone pulsed steadily, stronger than before. Jack bit back his apprehension and led them on, while the walls grew narrower still until his shoulders scraped against them on either side.

'We can't go much further,' Corriwen said. 'It's getting too narrow.'

'I can feel the ground shake,' Kerry said. 'That can't be good.'

Jack had felt the tremors underfoot. He prayed that they would get through this before the roof came down and buried them all. He forced his feet to keep walking until a blast of hot air came barrelling at them from ahead and snuffed the lamp out.

Darkness engulfed them and Jack felt a powerful sense of claustrophobia. The scorched air buffeted them and passed on. For a second there was silence, followed by an odd rasping sound, like hoarse whispers in the distance.

'Light,' Jack hissed. 'We need light.'

A spark told him Kerry's flint lighter was doing its best and then flame whooshed into life. He re-lit the lamp. Jack turned to lead on and they stepped out of the tunnel into a new chamber.

Fine gauzy threads scraped past Jack's face, snagging stickily on his skin. All around, filaments stretched in zig-zag patterns, a cat's cradle of strings that criss-crossed from wall to wall and ceiling to floor. Jack touched one and it stuck to his hand like glue. He tugged hard and it yielded, stretching the other threads in soft vibrations of sound.

Above them something scraped on stone. Corriwen raised the lamp and looked up.

Four pairs of red eyes reflected the tiny flame. Pin-points in the shadows.

'Oh, Jack,' Kerry whispered. 'I know what that is.'

'What?'

Before Kerry could reply, the eyes moved – and fast. Something the size of a rat bounded along a silken thread, making it twang as it moved. Jack glimpsed a number of pinioning legs and before he could yell a warning, a huge spider leapt from the web and landed on Corriwen's head.

Her scream of horror cut Jack like a knife. He had never heard Corriwen scream like that before.

For an instant Jack was rooted to the spot. He saw the spider's legs flex as it raised a grotesque head. He saw two yellow curves below the four eyes as it braced itself to strike.

Corriwen whirled and her free hand swung up to bat the thing away.

'Get it off me! Get it *off*!'

Her desperate cry broke Jack's paralysis. The great sword shot out before he even knew he had moved and sliced the bloated spider in half with one clean sweep just before the fangs could plunge into Corriwen's eyes.

Corriwen shuddered and stumbled back, tangled in a strand which broke from its anchor on the wall and whipped round her leg, sending her sprawling. The whole web thrummed like a bass string, making all the thick threads vibrate in unison.

Overhead, what looked like thin twigs waved in the air from hollows in the stonework. Jack saw them and snatched at Corriwen's hand, dragging her upright. The web was still snagged round her ankle and as she moved, it set up a strange harmonic in the strings.

'Are you okay?' Jack asked.

'I've had better days,' she gasped. 'But I'll live.'

'Don't worry,' Kerry snorted, trying to sound less afraid. 'They're only bugs.'

Above his head two of the thin twigs curved down to tap rhythmically on the web. Then something even bigger than the first hauled out from its hole in the stone, fangs dripping. Another monstrous spider launched itself, swinging on its own silk, eyes as red as flame.

It lurched across the web. Jack recoiled when he saw the fat body, trailing sticky lines. On the opposite side, two more emerged, and came scrabbling towards them.

Corriwen slashed at the web. It took two swings to cut through the sticky line. Kerry jabbed his sword at the scuttling spider, but it dodged to the side as if it read his mind. It landed above his head then pounced, faster than the eye could follow. Jointed legs snagged on either side of his shoulders. Kerry yelped and threw his shoulders against the wall, hoping to crush the thing, but just as quickly it crawled onto his head, holding tight with hairy legs.

Corriwen's knife flashed in front of Kerry's eyes and split the thing's pulsing abdomen. A spray of fine silk hosed out. She swung again and the knife cut straight through the narrow waist, and the spider dropped like a melon to splatter on the floor.

She glanced at Kerry. His face was white, but he managed a half-smile and gave her a thumbs up.

'Spiderwoman saves the day!'

'Only bugs!' she retorted, stepping close to give him a quick peck on the nose. 'You're all bluff and bravado.'

'Back!' Jack yelled. His sword cut an arc in the air, slicing through the web. It parted with a snap and two spiders catapulted off. Kerry speared one on the point of his blade. The other disappeared into the shadows.

'Back where?' Corriwen asked. She looked around wildly, searching for a way to escape, but there were no exits.

'We have to get out.' Rionna cried. She was unarmed and defenceless. Now there were hordes of spiders all over the web, and more emerging from holes, a mass of scuttling legs and glittering eyes.

Then a truly monstrous spider came scrambling down the wall, eyes glaring, fangs up and ready to strike. It was knee-high and covered in spiked hairs.

Jack braced himself to meet it head on. The heartstone kicked against his breast.

He slashed the great blade down. The creature dodged it, quick as a flash. It launched itself into the air. Jack managed to hit it with the flat of the sword and it thudded against the wall, bounced and came straight at Kerry, who ducked in pure reflex. As it flew over him, it trailed a skein of wet web which dropped around his shoulders. Then the spider swung in a circle, wrapping Kerry's head in a mass of sticky threads.

Jack dashed forward, trying to stab, while the thing spun round and around until Kerry's head was shrouded and his muffled cry could hardly be heard. Jack paused, waiting for a chance to kill it without harming Kerry, as the heartstone's pure note sang out.

Then another sound, even more powerful and clear, soared to overwhelm the heartstone. The walls shuddered and Jack felt the floor shiver under his feet.

Rionna was standing stock still, hands clamped against her temples, her eyes screwed tightly shut. Her mouth was open wide and the sound of her song vibrated the walls.

When the clear note rose to a crescendo, the big spider twitched and then it froze, still hunched on Kerry's back, fangs an inch from his neck. In a split second of clarity Jack lunged past Kerry's head, stabbing right between those fangs, straight and true, up to the hilt.

As Jack pushed Kerry to the side, he felt an acid bite as the spider-blood sprayed across the skin of his arm. With a desperate effort, he spun around, dragging the spider away. It flew off the sword and hit the wall with a pulpy crack then fell dead.

Beside him, Jack saw Corriwen's blades flicker as she jabbed and slashed, right and left, quick and expert, making each thrust count. Kerry got back to his feet, clawed at the web around his face until he was free and took a huge breath of air. When he stopped panting he swung again and lashed out in fury, scattering the creatures all around.

Rionna's song soared to a peak, and in front of her, Jack saw the walls shimmer in and out of focus, like ripples on water.

Suddenly she dashed forward and grabbed Corriwen's wrist.

'Come on,' she cried. 'There's no time.'

Rionna dragged Corriwen with her, heading straight for the wavering wall. It seemed to swallow them in the blink of an eye.

Jack swung his blade, clearing a path through the wave of monstrous spiders. He hacked at the webs until he reached the spot where Corriwen and Rionna had vanished, turned and hauled at Kerry and they both slumped against the wall.

Everything went black as they fell into it.

TWENTY ONE

The heat was so intense Jack could feel the hairs on his knuckles twist as they scorched.

Gouts of flame spurted up around them and the blast-furnace roar was louder than any jet engine Jack had ever heard. Black fumes clogged their throats and lungs as they dodged pillars of fire, stumbling, half-blinded, choking and coughing.

'Where are we now?' Kerry rasped. Corriwen was bent over in a fit of coughing. Jack held her arm.

'I don't know where this is,' Rionna admitted. 'I had no time to seek a haven. I sang blind and here we are.'

Pillars of fire rose to a blinding white as they watched, then faded to orange before roaring back up to full height and heat as if some monstrous bellows deep underground were pumping in and out.

Beyond where they stood, Jack noticed a fissure which split the chamber from floor to ceiling. With every pulse of flame, billowing smoke was sucked into it. It had to lead somewhere, he thought. Anywhere would be better than this.

He pulled the others close so they could hear him above the noise, but even then he had to shout. 'I think there's a way out. When the flare dies down, we can get through that crack.'

'Let's go for it then.' Kerry looked Jack in the eye. 'Just don't get it wrong, or we're toast.'

Jack stood up and told Corriwen to hold on to his sword-belt. Rionna gripped Corriwen's cape. Kerry had nothing to hold on to, but he stayed only a step behind.

As the flare reached its peak, Jack started running. For one moment it looked as though he would crash straight into the pillar of fire, but when he was only steps away from the searing heat, the flame shrank back down into the vent. Jack had timed it exactly right. He leapt over it, dragging Corriwen with him. Rionna was swung off her feet. Kerry snatched the neck of her tunic in mid-leap and held her like a rag-doll.

Blistering heat struck Jack's face in a wave. Kerry heard a blast of flame explode behind him as he ran after the others. Hot air pushed all of them faster into the fissure until it abruptly widened and they stumbled out, breathless and relieved.

'That was too close,' Kerry gasped. 'I think my backside's barbecued.'

'But we made it,' Jack said, knowing that if his timing

had been one second out, they wouldn't have.

'Made it to where?' Corriwen asked. Jack turned to see where she was looking. They were in a vast cavern. In its centre three colossal pillars stood in a triangle and on top of them, like a tabletop, lay a massive flat stone.

Underneath it, a profound swirling darkness.

High above them, Jack could see a mass of what looked like cloud or smoke turning in a slow circle like the eye of a storm. Bolts of lightning sparked within it. Kerry walked forward.

A sudden gust of wind struck them hard. Corriwen was knocked off her feet before anyone had a chance to grab her hand. Jack and Rionna were bowled after her, but Kerry managed to snag his fingers in a crack and held on. Corriwen slammed into him, then Jack and Rionna, but still Kerry held on with such desperate tenacity that he saved them all from being dragged off into the shrieking gale.

The storm overhead continued to spin in a dark spiral as they clung to Kerry until the wind began to abate and they were able to stand.

Kerry finally loosened his grip, wincing, but not complaining. Jack touched his shoulder gratefully. Kerry winked, grinned, and blew on his fingers.

Corriwen helped Rionna to her feet and looked across the cavern.

'Look there!' She pointed to the far side of the great chamber.

Shimmering lines of blue light spread filaments of

luminescence on the rock wall. From the centre of the light, a figure emerged, walking slowly. From her posture, even at that distance, Jack recognised Megrin and relief surged through him.

Then he saw what she was up against.

Megrin was holding her staff raised high in both hands as she walked towards the stone table in the centre of the room. Its carved head flickered as blinding shards of lightning forked towards her from the vortex. Megrin didn't flinch, but held her staff steady and the deadly bolts struck an invisible barrier above her head.

The smell of scorched stone drifted thick on the air. Kerry sneezed violently and held a hand over his nose.

'You come to your doom, witch.' A voice so loud and deep it made the rock resonate.

'And still I come,' Megrin's reply came clear and strong. 'I will not leave until I have what you have stolen from Uaine.'

'You will never leave this place, spellbinder. This is your final destination.'

'Show yourself. Your tricks could not stop me before. Nor will they now.'

He laughed. An unseen presence, but his laugh was powerful and vicious.

'Where is he?' Corriwen asked, scanning the chamber. On its chain around Jack's neck, the heartstone was thrumming once more. He could hear it loud in his head and knew that he was walking into danger. His hand found the hilt of the sword and gripped tight.

Megrin strode forward serenely, towards the stone table.

Between the upright pillars, Jack caught a movement. The dark underneath the table-stone swirled and from its depths another figure appeared.

He was tall, much taller than Megrin, and thin, and he clutched a long black staff. His face was hidden in deep shadows under a cowl, but his hands showed white as bone. He reminded Jack of Fainn the mad spellbinder of Wolfen Castle, and not only in his appearance. Jack sensed evil radiate from him, and an absence of any human quality.

At once Jack understood what Rionna had meant. This might have been her father once, but what he was now, Jack couldn't begin to guess.

Megrin's adversary remained in the shadow under the stone as she approached. He raised a thin hand and pointed his forefinger. They heard him chant a string of guttural words. Thunder exploded and Megrin was blasted backwards off her feet. Before she could react, the ground around her began to writhe and buckle. The stone mounds swelled and elongated into slender shapes. They branched at their tips and began to flex.

'Hands!' Jack heard the disbelief in Corriwen's voice.

But they *were* hands. Hands of moving stone that reached for Megrin, pinioning her arms and legs, smothering her in their grip.

'We have to help her,' Corriwen cried. Before Jack could stop her she was running towards Megrin, but he knew it was the wrong thing to do. They needed to stop for a moment and think, but Corriwen had forced his hand. She was twenty paces away before he reacted and then he too was running, drawing the great sword as he hared after her.

As Jack and Corriwen ran across the chamber, Kerry saw the cowled figure turn towards him and Rionna. Its black staff pointed directly at them. Something sizzled past his ear and hit the wall behind them. Kerry turned to take Rionna's hand and follow Jack and Corrie.

Then he saw Rionna's face was white with shock. He stopped and looked up in alarm.

A tall shadow oozed from the stone wall, taking shape as it approached. Kerry saw a wizened woman in tattered rags reach to take Rionna by the shoulders. A face as dry and cracked as old parchment bent towards her.

'My little girl,' it said in a voice like shifting sand. 'Come back to find your mother.'

Kerry saw that what he had first thought were deep-set eyes were not eyes at all, just sunken pits in a crumbling skull. Hanks of straggly grey hair had fallen off in patches and stuck to its mouldering hood. The hands were long and skeletal, covered in a thin membrane that looked as if it would flake to powder at a touch.

'Good child . . .' it hissed. 'Loving child.'

Rionna stood frozen in horror. The apparition drew her into its embrace.

'Come and love your mother, child. Be with me now.'

Rionna's knees buckled and her body slumped. For a moment Kerry was too stunned to move as he saw Rionna's cheeks draw into hollows. Her skin seemed to dry out like a fallen leaf in hot sun.

A huge anger, more powerful than any he had felt in his life, surged through him. She had saved his life and she had brought them all together again. And she was the only other human being, apart from Jack and Corriwen, who thought he was worth anything at all.

'Get your hands off her!'

Kerry leapt forward, drawing his short-sword in one practised motion. He angled the point upwards and thrust straight-armed.

The blade went through the creature with hardly any resistance at all. Dry dust puffed out where the sword had pierced. Kerry drew back and stabbed again. The monstrosity turned its peeling face towards him and its mouth opened, showing a black hole lined with long, brown teeth. Rionna's breathing sounded ragged and desperate as the spectre drew her closer still.

'I said . . .' He stabbed again, and again and again. 'Leave . . . her . . . *alone!*'

The mangy cloak was puckered with holes, but Kerry's attack appeared to have had no other effect. It was still turned towards him, sunken sockets regarding him mercilessly. Rionna was sagging, disappearing into the tatters and Kerry suddenly knew that if this thing enveloped her, she'd be lost forever.

Suddenly a long arm snapped out and bony fingers clenched around his throat.

Kerry gasped as his breath was cut off and he was swung right off his feet. The sword spun from his hand and clanged on the floor. The hand drew him forward, up close to the glaring skull. He could hear the blood pounding in his ears as the fingers squeezed tight. He smelled musty dry rot and mould. Up this close, he could see that dusty cobwebs hung from the straggly hair. The grip tightened and he felt his vision begin to waver. The mouth opened even wider, mere inches away from his eyes.

Kerry panicked, helpless in the inexorable grasp. His hands flailed for anything to use to break free. He fumbled in his pocket, wishing he had his penknife, or a rock, or *anything*. All he found was the little lighter that he'd used to light the lamp in the tunnel. Like a drowning man, he clutched at it. Maybe he could jam it in the eye socket.

Instinct took over. His thumb found the little wheel and snapped down. Sparks jumped. A whoosh of flame leapt from his fingers and raced up the tattered threads of its cloak.

In an instant, the creature's shoulders and cowl were wreathed in crackling fire. Flames stuttered along the sleeve of the hand that held him by the throat, and suddenly he was falling free. He landed on his feet, spun towards the burning shape, ignoring the sudden heat and snatched at Rionna's almost-hidden form. His fingers found her slender arms and he threw them both to the side while the creature spun faster and faster, hissing like a steam vent and collapsing in on itself as the updraught fanned the flames.

Rionna shivered against him, and he held her tight as she gasped great breaths and warmth began to return to her body. Then she burst into sudden tears.

'Don't,' Kerry said hoarsely. His throat felt as if it had been squeezed flat. 'That wasn't your mother.'

She sobbed against him.

'It's a trick,' he insisted. 'It's all a trick. You said yourself ... it gets in your head and twists everything.'

He felt her nod her agreement into the curve of his neck.

'Don't worry, I won't let anything happen to you. Cross my heart and hope to die.'

She raised her head to look at him with those luminous eyes. Before either of them could speak, on the far side of the chamber Corriwen Redthorn screamed like a banshee.

Jack and Corriwen ran a murderous gauntlet towards Megrin, blasted by jagged shrapnel as bolts of lightning struck the ground around them. The stone hands were dragging Megrin into the ground. She desperately reached for her staff, but it lay just beyond her grasp.

Without thinking, Corriwen launched herself at the mass of stone imprisoning Megrin and began to hammer at the rocky fingers with the hilt of her knife. Jack went to retrieve the staff, but it spun away and he stumbled.

It rolled further away from him, then rose into the air, spinning slowly as it gained height and floated towards the darkness underneath the table-stone.

Bodron beckoned silently and Megrin's staff soared towards him. In seconds it would be within his grasp.

He didn't know what might happen if Bodron were to get his hands on the staff, but Jack knew it wouldn't be good. He had to do something, and fast.

On top of the stone slab, something polished reflected dazzling light back into his eyes. He screwed his eyes against the glare and ran for Megrin's staff.

Corriwen saw a streak of motion as she fought to free Megrin. One second Jack was turning. The next he was a blur, given miraculous speed by Rune's boots. He leapt for the staff, hands stretched above him. She saw his fingers snatch at it in the air.

Jack's whole body shuddered as he grabbed the staff just before Bodron could reach it. A huge shock ran through him and he almost lost his grip on it.

Corriwen heard his cry of surprise and pain, and saw him fall to the ground, the staff firmly clenched in both hands.

The hooded figure roared in fury.

TWENTY TWO

Jack's knees buckled as he hit the ground. Bodron roared again, and the cavern walls shook. He pointed his black staff and forks of orange light stabbed towards Jack, who twisted and rolled as the flares exploded around him. Megrin's staff bucked and juddered in his grasp as it dragged him forward. The friction burned the skin of his hands, but he held on tight. Corriwen screamed a warning as Jack tried to dig his heels in the ground, straining against the force that pulled him inexorably towards where Bodron waited in the shadow.

Skeletal fingers reached towards him, but not for Megrin's staff.

As Jack tried to squirm away he felt the heartstone on its chain slip from his tunic. Whatever power Bodron exerted on Jack was also pulling the stone, for it had swung out, almost a foot away from Jack's face. Bodron's eyes blazed like headlights and Jack saw that though he might have human shape, those eyes burned with hell-fire.

'Bring it to me!' The glee in Bodron's voice was unmistakeable.

'Never!' Jack grated. He groaned with the strain as he tried to pull back, fumbling desperately for the great sword hilt. He would never give up his father's heartstone. Not without a fight.

Kerry had been through enough adventures with his friend to know that if Bodron got hold of the Journeyman's heartstone, everything was lost.

Jack Flint was the best friend he had ever had. The best *anybody* ever had. He had saved Kerry's life a dozen times or more. And Kerry had come through the gate to Uaine because he didn't want Jack Flint to face danger alone. If Jack ever needed him, he needed him *now*.

As he ran towards where Jack struggled, Kerry scooped up a heavy piece of rock. With his free hand he unshipped his sling from his belt, fitted the rock in the cradle and swung it around his head.

He braced himself, torqued his shoulders and launched the stone with all his strength.

Kerry was still running. He could hear Corriwen yelling but he ignored her and threw himself headlong at Jack in a flying tackle that knocked him sideways. Jack landed hard, with Kerry on top of him. Megrin's staff was jarred from his grip and tumbled away. As they disentangled themselves, two pale shapes resolved into two white goshawks that swooped down, talons agape, and seized it.

The rock took Bodron between the eyes. He staggered backwards, arms flailing and as he stumbled into the shadow he lost his grip on the black staff.

Corriwen and Rionna watched in amazement as the darkness under the stone enveloped Bodron, folding around him until he vanished from sight. The ground heaved.

What Corriwen saw coming out of the shadow made her scream.

Both Jack and Kerry turned and froze.

The dark mass under the table-stone had become shapes from Jack's deepest nightmares. In an instant he was catapulted back once more to the memory of a desperate race through the forest, as a baby in his father's arms, while pale-eyed shadows hounded them towards the homeward gate.

'What in the name of . . .' Kerry started.

Eyes fixed on them hungrily. Long arms reached out. Two-clawed toes scrabbled on stone.

Nightshades.

Behind them, Bodron emerged from the enfolding dark and Jack saw that he had changed utterly. He loomed twice as tall. His face was contorted, his skin swelling and puckering as if something inside was trying to get out. Under the cowl his eyes were aflame.

'Journeyman,' Bodron's voice rumbled. He pointed a long finger at Jack. 'Journeyman's whelp. I destroyed your father long ago and sent him where none return. But you bear that which I desire. Give it to me now and you might still have life, of a kind.'

A fierce anger erupted in Jack's chest. This beast was responsible for it all. The loss of his father; the years of uncertainty and mystery. And the darkness that infested Uaine. Before he could spit out a response, Bodron spoke again.

'Or else my nightshades will feast, and I will have it then.'

'Not a chance,' Kerry cried. 'You'll have to take it from his cold, dead hands. If you can!'

'Thanks, Kerry,' Jack muttered.

'No problem. I heard it in a movie. The good guys won.'

The demon rumbled once more. 'Deny me and suffer forever. It was I who sent the nightshades to herd you to the stone gates. It was I who brought you here. You are mine.'

Jack drew the great sword, unsure whether it would be of any use as Bodron and the shades stalked towards them.

'I came here of my own free will,' he cried, quivering, not with fear, but anger. 'You didn't bring me. The Sky Queen sent me. I came to find my father. But now I am here to take my revenge for what you have done.'

The heartstone throbbed violently. Jack's sword was in his hands and surging with its own life.

'You are *nothing*. You don't belong in *any* world.'

He and Kerry stood shoulder to shoulder. Kerry reached out a hand and clasped his arm.

As the nightshades stalked towards them, Kerry squeezed Jack's arm tight, a gesture of solidarity. 'Come on. We're in a corner. The only way out is to do it to them before they do it to us.'

'The only way,' Jack repeated, nodding. His chin was set, knuckles white.

Suddenly, behind Jack and Kerry, something exploded. Jack spun around, ready to defend himself when he saw Megrin on her feet. Her face was expressionless and calm.

The stone hands that had pinned her down were flying away in fragments. She had her staff in her hands and blue fire ran up and down its length. The two white birds wheeled above her.

Corriwen knelt on one knee. She drew Jack's amberhorn bow back as she searched for a target. Before she could shoot, Megrin touched her on the shoulder and made a sign over Jack's quiver of black arrows. A dazzling light arced between the staff and the obsidian arrowheads.

'Fight darkness with light,' she said softly. 'It is always so.'

Corriwen nodded. She drew back until the feather-flights brushed her cheek and let loose. A blue streak flashed between Jack and Kerry as the arrow took the nearest nightshade in its bulging eye. It screamed. Black fumes poured out from its eye and its head melted like tar.

Jack sprang into action, slashing his sword right and left. As he sliced down on the crown of the nearest nightshade, it felt as if he hit solid stone, but the blade didn't falter. It made a sickly crunch and drove right down between the eyes. The two halves of the hideous head fell apart like a cut fruit.

Kerry tried to launch a heavy rock but as he swung back, a claw reached for him and grabbed his wrist with inhuman strength. A shock of cold rippled up his arm. Jack whirled to help him and in one fluid motion, severed the claw that gripped Kerry's arm, then spun away to face the rest of them. Kerry sank to his knees as the cold surged through his veins.

Rionna rushed to him, oblivious to the danger. She snatched the claw that still gripped Kerry's arm, tugged it free and let it drop to the ground. It hit with a wet splat and collapsed into shiny black rivulets that soaked into cracks in the stone. She put her arms round Kerry's chest and tried to drag him away.

Bodron suddenly leapt at them and his hand clamped on Rionna's head. He lifted her effortlessly up to his eye level.

Jack desperately slashed at the nightshades. From beyond the melée, Corriwen launched arrow after arrow, and he began to think they might have a chance.

But now he was backed into a corner, jabbing and hacking and with every strike the nightshades shrank back only a little, and then surged forward, barricading him tightly against the chamber wall.

Corriwen stopped shooting. Despite her skill with the bow, there was now too much of a risk of hitting Jack as the nightshades crowded in on him. She drew both knives and ran forward to fight by his side, but before she reached him, they suddenly pushed forward until Jack was completely lost from view.

Jack was surrounded by glaring eyes and hooking claws, squeezed in tight against the stone and without enough space to swing the sword. A long, bony claw reached for the heartstone.

Reacting on instinct Jack leapt, and Corriwen saw him appear suddenly over the mass of attackers as they closed in. Thin arms, quick as striking snakes, tried to hook him from the air, but not quick enough. One claw shot out, but it only snagged the satchel that swung from Jack's shoulders. Something ripped, but his momentum powered him on.

Rune's boots made Jack fly like an acrobat, tumbling through the air. The sword-blade reflected the blue and orange light from where Megrin and Bodron were locked together.

Jack landed, light as a cat. He turned fast, expecting to see nightshades surging after him and it took him a second to realise that he was not on the ground. He could see Megrin and Bodron far below him. Corriwen was running towards Kerry and Rionna. Jack was high above them, high on the flat table-stone supported by the three immense rock pillars.

Whatever had almost blinded him before now glinted in the corner of his vision and when he turned he saw a circle of burnished metal pages each etched with intricate figures and strange script.

The Copperplates. He knew they could be nothing else.

They blazed with supernatural power. Twenty-one gleaming plates of copper. Not standing, but somehow hovering in a perfect circle. Directly above them, the dark storm continued to spin slowly, crackling with lightning.

Jack stepped towards the centre of the table-stone.

Corriwen reached Kerry and Rionna. She pointed up at the great table-stone.

As Kerry and Rionna raised their heads, they saw Jack high above them. He was holding the great sword out in front of him. Around him, polished metal gleamed. They saw him walk forward, towards the centre of the stone.

And then he disappeared completely.

TWENTY THREE

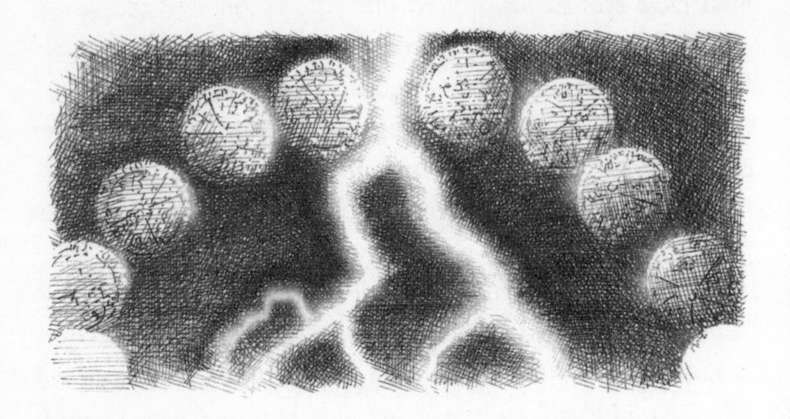

The Copperplates hung suspended in the air. The beauty of the gleaming metal plates and the intricate patterns etched on their surfaces drew him to their core. He was helpless to resist.

Everything beyond the Copperplates faded away. He could sense immense power surging around him.

Jack looked at the surface of one of the plates. For an instant he saw himself reflected in its depths and his vision blurred. He felt a sudden dizzy sensation and without warning blinding pain exploded between his eyes. He cried out as everything went black.

He floated up to the surface, struggling for breath. Behind him the falls of Temair thundered to foam. He gasped a breath and went under again, searching for Kerry who had fallen with him. Down into the depths he swam, while slender creatures with wide eyes swam around and he felt amongst the weeds until he found something. He grabbed at it, pulled himself lower …

Kerry's pale face swayed in the current, mouth wide, eyes colourless, staring at him with contempt.

Jack jerked back in horror, swallowed a mouthful of bitter water …

… and he was on the shifting slab on the brimstone flow in Temair's badlands. Corriwen reached for his hand to help him but he didn't risk taking it and she slipped backwards into the fire. Steam hissed and he saw her flesh burn away as she sank into it until all he could see were her accusing eyes …

He cringed from the sight, then found himself at the bottom of the stairwell in the Major's house back home. The Major's shotgun lay rusted beside a pile of bones. A skull glared blindly at him, and a babble of voices clamoured in his head.

'You let me drown!' Kerry's voice was cold and watery.

'No! I'd never let you!' *The words formed in Jack mind but wouldn't come out.*

'You could have saved me …' Corriwen was a whisper in his ear.

'Please. No!'

'You brought the darkness into my home …' The Major accused him.

Jack moaned and clapped his hands over his ears to banish

the voices. Something punched him in the belly. Punched again. Hit a third time.

His eyes opened ...

And he was out of the nightmare, still on the table-stone. Now the Copperplates were spinning around Jack in a slow circle, like parts of a gleaming carousel, matching the storm overhead.

A fourth blow to the stomach almost knocked the wind from him and he raised himself up.

His satchel was jerking violently, kicking hard just under his ribs. The straps had worked themselves loose.

Another nightmare, Jack told himself. Rionna had explained that the dark power fed on the fear it created in human minds. Within the ring of the Copperplates, that power seemed magnified a hundredfold. It had reached into his mind, seeking out his worst terrors, and made them real.

Whatever controlled these ancient talismans had the power to drive a world to the edge of madness.

At the edge of his vision, the gargoyle creatures were now clambering over the rim of the table-stone. The nightshades had found him.

He was trapped. As the Copperplates spun around him, he realised he was helpless. Jack sank to his haunches, sword drawn, ready to roll under the whirling plates and fight to the end. As he did so, his bag bucked again.

The *Book of Ways* tumbled out. Its old leather cover flipped open.

Without warning, the whirling Copperplates broke formation. Overhead a jagged fork of lightning stabbed into the stone. Jack was almost hurled off his feet. One plate came slashing towards him. He rolled and it sliced barely an inch past his head. Thrown off balance, Jack tried to steady himself. His hand found the *Book of Ways*.

The heartstone throbbed with a power that surged through Jack and arced between his fingers and the pages of the book.

Another of the Copperplates lanced in at him, straight at his eyes.

The book bucked in his hands, pages whirring, but he was hardly aware of it as the Copperplate spun in like a blade whistling towards him through the air.

Before he could move, the *Book of Ways* leapt up and snapped shut on it with a sound like a hammer-blow. The force pushed Jack backwards, but he held on to the book's spine. It bucked again, almost throwing him off balance and when it opened again, Jack saw a flash of gold that quickly faded to white. The Copperplate's symbols stood out starkly on the page and then sank into the surface, leaving it clean and white again.

The book suddenly felt heavy in his hands, as if it had absorbed a great weight. Jack's fingers tingled. Another Copperplate came streaking towards him. The book opened to meet it and it vanished into the snapping pages.

One by one, while thunder roared and nightshades hovered, ready to pounce, the spinning Copperplates whirred in at Jack and the book rose to meet them and swallow them in its pages.

When it had captured the last of them, the book's weight forced Jack to his knees. For one last time, the cover opened again, the old pages blazing with pure white light. The book lifted from his hands as it shot out a blinding beam which speared upwards towards the centre of the swirling black storm overhead.

For a second, the air around him seemed to crystallise. Then the whole world exploded.

The nightshades disappeared in a blast of intense heat. Huge stalactites lanced down from the roof and shattered to a million flying shards. Jack looked up and saw an enormous spear of rock coming straight for him. He jerked backwards and it struck the table-stone with such force the platform cracked in two.

He felt the whole structure tilt slowly and leapt off the stone, sword in one hand, book in the other and landed on solid ground as the megalith collapsed. All around the great chamber, the rock walls began to melt and flow.

Bodron screamed in impotent fury. Behind him, the table-stone slumped into the dark pit below. From every fissure in the shattered rock of the great cavern, shadows streamed out and flowed into the ever widening crater.

Jack's sword vibrated in harmony with the heartstone's steady pulse. He ran to where Kerry was huddled with Corriwen and Rionna as huge stones tumbled from on high to be swallowed by the dark.

Megrin was chanting now, her green eyes locked on Bodron's.

'Back to the pit where you belong!' Her voice gained strength. 'Beast of the darkness. And never return to the world of light!'

'Hag! I will take you with me,' Bodron roared. His eyes blazed as he raised his staff.

Jack saw his chance. This was the beast, the demon that had killed his father; the monster that had sent the nightshades after them.

As he started forward, Kerry realised what he was about to attempt and tried to hold him back. Jack twisted out of his grip. He leapt over mounds of fallen stone, dodging tumbling rocks, his eyes fixed on the demonic face.

The sword flashed as Jack thrust upwards and stabbed with all his strength. The blade went through the black cloak, up under the ribs until its bloodied point came through the shoulder of Bodron's raised arm. The black staff fell to the ground.

Bodron's burning eyes widened in shock and surprise. They turned away from Megrin and swung down to where Jack stood, both hands on the sword's hilt. Then they fixed on him with such malevolence and hatred that Jack felt it shudder through him.

But it was too late. Bodron sagged to the ground. All the life-force was draining out of him. His cowl slipped back and Jack was close enough to see a wizened face with sparse white hair and eyes sunk deep into hollows.

He turned his head to look beyond Jack and his eyes found Rionna's but there was no recognition in them. The ground lurched again and the darkness from the pit expanded outwards to swallow Bodron completely.

As Jack ran back to the others, the ground began to fall away and suddenly there was nothing solid under their feet.

He tried to stab the sword into the ground to stop them from slipping, but Kerry slid into him, dragging Rionna with him. Corriwen lost her footing and they slid together towards the yawning crater.

Megrin was too far away to help. She saw the darkness expand and consume them. In one last desperate act she threw her staff with all her strength. It soared up and plummeted into the centre of the black maelstrom into which her young friends were disappearing.

There was a blinding flash and the rock walls all around disintegrated and turned to dust. To Megrin's amazement, the black hole began to close. In an instant it shrank to a single point, then it shut completely. All noise died.

Megrin found herself standing alone on a barren moorland in the far west of Uaine. Above her, the sky was clear and blue and the sun shone bright and warm.

There was no sign of Jack Flint, Kerry Malone or Corriwen Redthorn, or of her niece, Bodron's daughter, Rionna.

TWENTY FOUR

They all fell together. If they screamed, none heard it. To Jack it seemed as if they fell forever.

His last memory was a wide circle of light racing away from him at astonishing speed until it was just a dot which vanished in an instant.

Faster and faster they spun, clinging desperately to one another, down and down and down. The darkness pressed hard on them. The air grew thick so that it was almost impossible to breathe. Jack felt his consciousness fade.

Some time later he awoke, still holding Corriwen's hand, still falling, but now they were descending fast on a steep slope as smooth as glass. It took Jack a little while to realise that he was awake, and not in the middle of some nightmare, and when he realised that they were sliding, he tried to dig his heels in to slow his momentum.

Nothing happened. He stabbed down with the sword-blade, holding it like an ice-pick. Its point sent out a blaze of sparks as it cut a furrow in the surface, slowing them just a little.

As they slid further the glassy surface became grainy, like fine sand. Jack forced the blade in harder and gradually their speed diminished as the slope began to level out.

Eventually they ground to a halt, surrounded by the dust kicked up by their passage. Here, everything was silent. Some distance away, in the direction they had been travelling, Jack could make out a deep, ominous red glow. It was the only light he could see.

Gingerly, he got to his feet and sheathed the sword. He helped Corriwen up, feeling as if his whole body was covered in bruises. Kerry rolled over and he and Rionna managed to stand. Every footstep sent up a cloud of fine dust that smelt of old cinders.

'What happened?' Kerry asked groggily.

'The ground opened,' Corriwen said. 'It sucked us down. Jack was on the stone. Everything flashing around him.'

'The Copperplates,' Rionna said.

Jack nodded. 'The book swallowed them. I don't know how.'

Corriwen touched him on the shoulder. 'You faced that thing, Jack. I saw you. You're the Journeyman for certain.'

Before Jack could respond, Kerry piped up. 'I'm not even going to ask where we are, but I don't like it already. It stinks.'

'At least we're alive,' Corriwen said.

'Don't be so sure,' Kerry mumbled, breaking into a fit of coughing as the dust rasped his throat.

'We fell a long way into the pit,' Rionna said. 'This must be the nether-lands, the realm of the nightshades. I read my father's old scripts. This seems to fit.'

'Bodron used the Copperplates to open the Dark Way. The book stopped them doing any more harm.' Jack patted the satchel. 'It's got power of its own.'

'So can it get us out of here?'

'I don't know,' Jack said honestly. He believed Rionna's explanation, but he still wasn't sure exactly where they were. In his heart, he was sure he had led them to the end of the road, and the end of his quest. Bodron had destroyed his father. Now, thanks to him they were all at the bottom of a fathomless pit.

It had all been for nothing. That realisation settled on him like a dead weight.

'Brilliant,' Kerry said with weary sarcasm. He began to lead the way down the slope, slip-sliding over shards of what looked like fire-blackened pottery, until they got near the base where the red glow was brighter.

'Aw, Jeez!'

Kerry held up something, and Jack realised that they had been sliding down neither shale nor pottery shards. In his hand Kerry held a skull fragment, the forehead and two empty sockets. They were at the bottom of a vast hill of crushed and broken bones.

Jack shuddered. There was no way any of them wanted to climb back up that slope. He moved to lead them towards the red glow in the distance when a high-pitched noise from above stopped him in his tracks. He looked up into the darkness. The sound grew louder and higher, like a siren. Something sparked brightly as it fell towards them. Jack pulled Corriwen aside. Kerry snatched at Rionna, but she held her ground as the mysterious light plunged towards her.

At the last second she raised both hands and caught Megrin's staff.

Faint blue fire still rippled along its length. Its light reflected in her wide eyes.

Corriwen said, 'She must have dropped it.'

'Perhaps she closed the gate with it,' Rionna said. She planted the staff between her feet. 'Perhaps the sun now shines in Uaine.'

'That's all very well,' Kerry snorted. 'But it sure isn't shining down here.'

Jack said nothing. He was thinking. The Major had told him – and it seemed like years ago now – that there were no such things as coincidences, not in serious matters anyway. All of the wise folk they had met on their adventures had agreed on that.

Jack's eyes were fixed on Megrin's staff, which Rionna held in both hands. Now they had the staff, and whatever power it might have left in it.

It couldn't be a coincidence. There must, he told himself, be a purpose.

And if there was a purpose, then there was hope. Maybe . . .

Behind them, a vast mound of broken bones. Ahead, the eerie glow, and forward was the only direction they could take. The nearer they got to it, the thicker the fumes and the hotter it became.

As they came to the edge of a red pit, Jack realised there was nowhere further to go and his heart sank. It was vast, a great hole from which smoke belched and fires far below glowed like lava.

'This is it,' Kerry said, looking down at the fiery pit. 'Dead end.'

'There must be a way out,' Corriwen said, but her voice was far from certain. She looked at Jack for confirmation.

Jack drew the *Book of Ways* from his bag. He laid it flat on the ground and watched as it flipped open. As he had on the table-stone Jack caught a glint of coppery gold before the page turned white again.

The old script began to write itself on a blank page.

Far from all the worlds of man
Journeyman must venture on
Brave the fire in circles steep
Brave the dark in cavern deep
Two deadly trials must you face
Until you find the final place
To meet the doom so long foretold
Yet traveller must now be bold
Whence none returned to tell the tale

Kerry, Corriwen and Rionna looked at him, waiting for his reaction. Jack rubbed his chin, thinking. The book had confirmed one thing: Megrin's staff was here for a purpose.

'I don't like the none-returned part,' Kerry said.

'None returned *so far*,' Corriwen countered, with more confidence than she felt. 'We've won through until now, haven't we?'

'Well, I can't see a way out of here.'

Jack wasn't listening. The words were running through his head. It had told them to venture on, which meant they couldn't go back. But the last line kept repeating itself, like a mantra.

With heartstone, book and staff prevail.

There *must* be hope, he told himself. There must. Jack edged towards the rim of the fiery pit, holding his arm against his face to ward off the heat. He looked down.

Circles down.

He had to rub his eyes several times before he finally saw it. A narrow trackway made its way down in a spiral. It was little more than a ledge, but it followed the sides of the pit in a corkscrew shape into the depths. And just where it began to disappear into the fumes, Jack saw what he was looking for. A dark shape in the blasted stone. A hole in the rock. A cave. An exit?

He beckoned to Kerry. Corriwen and Rionna followed and Jack showed them the ledge and the hole in the cauldron wall.

'It's a chance,' he said. 'I don't know how good, but it's a chance. And I believe the book.'

'Me too,' Kerry said. 'But one slip and we're goners.'

'Just don't slip,' Corriwen warned him. 'Or there'll be trouble!'

'That's all the warning I need,' Kerry grinned. 'I'd rather face the fire.'

'Get serious,' Jack said. 'That's just what we have to do. And be careful.'

Jack led the descent, following the rim until they reached the narrow path. They made their way down, pressing themselves against the rock, both for safety and to shield themselves a little from the searing updraught of heat.

The distance was greater than it had appeared from above. It took more than an hour of slow progress to get down to the level of the fissure.

It was no natural cave. Two ancient pillars marked an entrance, or an exit. Once inside, the four of them walked until they were far enough from the direct heat to begin to cool a little. Corriwen heard the splash of water and followed the sound until she found a small pool.

All four of them got down on their knees and drank until they could drink no more. Kerry ducked his head right under until he needed to breathe and came up spluttering.

'I never tasted water as good as that in my whole life,' he declared. 'Even in Rionna's world.'

He was getting to his feet, when a voice boomed out without warning:

'*Who dares trespass?*'

Kerry got such a fright, he jerked back, missed his footing and fell on his backside into the middle of the pool.

Jack could hear breathing, rough and ragged as old leaking bellows, and wondered why none of them had noticed it before. A shape loomed some distance ahead of them.

'*Answer!*'

'We're just passing through,' Kerry said nervously.

'None traverse this low road.' The voice echoed from wall to wall. 'Save those who answer true.'

Jack edged forward. Corriwen was at his side. Rionna held the staff up. It glowed faintly, just enough to make out a shape in front of them, twice as tall as a man, but squat and rough, as though it might have been made of stone itself. Two great horns twisted over its hooded eyes.

'Who are you?' Jack asked. He stood at the edge of what seemed like another pit which yawned between them and the massive presence.

'I am the Crom Cruach. It is my doom to guard the low road. I judge who passes by, and who stays.'

'We can't stay,' Kerry piped up, shaking water from his boot. 'We're on a mission.'

'You are at the end of your journey, or the beginning. Answer three riddles and you may pass. Fail and you remain forever with the lost.'

With that, a grinding rumble came from behind them and when they turned in alarm, Jack saw the two pillars at the mouth of the cavern move slowly towards each other. It was clear now that they were not actually pillars, but the edges of two massive doors.

'Wait!'

'I wait for no mortal.'

'But you haven't asked the questions.'

'Ah, the impetuosity of man. I had forgotten the haste of mortals.'

The creature bent forward and now that his eyes had become accustomed to the gloom, Jack saw that it was not squatting as he had thought, but sitting hard against the cave wall. Both of its colossal arms were manacled to three heavy chains. Its moss-covered legs were pinioned to the rock floor by bands of stone. Whatever the Crom Cruach was, it was a prisoner here.

'Answer me right, and you may pass. Fail one and your journey ends here.'

'Go for it, Jack,' Kerry urged. 'You're the brains.'

A long silence followed, broken only by the ragged breathing of the Crom Cruach. Its head sunk to its chest, as if the horns were too heavy to carry. Then it spoke:

I always run, though lie abed.
My mouth is furthest from my head
The only time you see me still
Is in the grip of winter chill.

As the verse ended, the grinding sound started again behind them. Inch by inch, the doors began to crawl towards each other. It was like a clock ticking off the seconds. He closed his eyes, repeating the rhyme to himself over and over again. The heartstone pulsed warm in his grip.

When he opened his eyes, Kerry was looking at him with urgent expectancy.

Jack smiled confidently. 'You're a river. Always flowing. Under ice in winter. And the river mouth is at the sea, far from the headwaters.'

The grinding of the doors stopped. Kerry wiped sweat from his forehead.

The creature flexed huge muscles and heaved on the chain. They all looked and saw, rising up from the depths, a single black pillar a yard wide. It reached the height of the rim and stopped.

'It's a stepping stone,' Corriwen said.

'Only one,' Kerry observed. 'We need more than that.'

'We all have to think,' Jack said, 'and think hard. Don't just leave it up to me, because I could be wrong. And if I am, then we'll be stuck here. We have to get them right, every one, because that door will close anyway.'

The guardian leaned back against the wall, lowered its great head yet again. Its voice boomed out once more:

In poor man's green and drab I flee
To travel wide the distant sea
And after many season turns
In silver mail a king returns.

The doors began to grind together again. Jack gripped the heartstone, willing images to come. All he could see was Kerry, lying on his front beside the stream waiting for a fish to swim close. But there was nothing else. He tried to concentrate, read something into the picture.

Behind them the doors rumbled. Corriwen put an encouraging hand on his shoulder, but despite it, Jack could find no solution.

'Easy peasy,' Kerry snorted. 'Even I know that one.'

'Well, be quick,' Corriwen told him.

'I'm a fisherman, and you're a salmon, aren't you? You start out a little green parr and go off to sea, and come back a big silver king of the river.'

The doors halted again. The guardian began to haul on the second chain and inch by inch, another rose up from the darkness and locked into place. Between them, the darkness seemed to descend forever.

Kerry punched the air, grinning from ear to ear. Rionna grabbed his hand and held it tight.

Jack checked the doors. They were a mere yard apart. Next time they would meet each other and close the cave-mouth completely. Everything depended on the final question.

It came before he was ready for it:

If you give me, give me free
Yet in giving, still keep me
Trade me not for fame or token
Be unworthy if I'm broken.

'Jeez,' Kerry breathed. 'That's a tough one.'

Jack pressed the heartstone to his forehead, eyes closed in concentration. The seconds ticked away.

'Come on, Jack,' Kerry whispered. 'You can do it.'

The image that came was of Corriwen high in the cage of Wolfen Castle in Eirinn, when she had stood up for the boy who was her fellow captive. What that meant, he couldn't imagine. Nothing else would come.

Behind them, the doors crashed together. This was it. They were trapped. And Jack could not think of the answer to this riddle.

Corriwen touched him on the shoulder.

'I learnt at my father's knee,' she said, 'that to be a Redthorn is to be always true. True to your heart and true to your word.'

She turned to the creature on the far side of the chasm.

'You are a promise,' she called in a clear voice. 'A promise freely given and always kept. A promise never to be broken.'

For a long moment, the only sound was the rumbling breath in the shadows. Then they saw the great arms reach again and the chain groaned under the tension, link by link. A third pillar rose up from the depth of the pit.

They couldn't go back. They had only one choice.

'Come on!' Without a pause, Jack leapt onto the first pillar, and made it to the far side of the chasm. Corriwen followed, light as a cat. Kerry took Rionna's hand, and together they used the pillars as stepping stones.

The horned creature sat still, breathing raggedly. Up close, they could see it had a broad and bestial face. Its hands were huge and horny, but its great feet bore cloven hooves. There was a gap between it and the wall, leading to a narrow passage. It was the only way past.

'May we pass?' Jack thought he'd better ask.

'You answered,' it replied.

'Where does this lead?'

'To your doom, child. Doom for every mortal.' It sounded as old as time and very, very weary.

As they skirted past it, wary of those powerful hands that might reach out and smash them flat, the creature didn't even move. Behind them, the three pillars slowly sunk down out of sight and the chains rattled up again.

Kerry led the way to the passage, but Rionna paused beside the guardian. Two red eyes regarded her from a hideously wrinkled face.

'You are trapped here. How long?'

'So long, I have no memory of it.'

'Can't you break free?'

'If I could, I would. I long for movement.'

She turned to Jack. 'No creature should be chained.'

Jack looked at the clamps that pinned its legs to the floor. They were old and eroded, but still solid.

'If I help you, would you help us?'

'Help you? How?'

'We face another trial. Do you know what it is?' He drew the great sword. Before the thing could reply, Jack brought the blade down on the centre of the clamps. Sparks flew and the old stone broke into pieces.

The creature let out a long slow sigh. Its hooves scraped on the stone.

'So good! So good to move.' It swung its head towards him. 'Hear me now. Two brothers guard two doors. One door leads to burning fire. The other lets you pass. You may ask one question.'

'What question?'

'You decide. But be warned. One tells only the truth. The other only lies.'

'Brilliant,' Jack muttered under his breath. 'That's it?'

It stretched its legs out and brought them up again. Its eyes rolled beneath the twisted horns. It sighed again. 'So *good* to move.'

Jack and Rionna turned away and left the old monster to what ease it could find.

The brothers were not at all what Jack had expected. As the path descended further into the old rock, he explained to the others what the guardian had said.

'We have to think carefully. We only get one chance at this.'

'Doesn't sound very fair to me,' Kerry grumbled.

'This is not a place of fairness,' Rionna said. 'We are beyond the good in the Underplace.'

'Well, the big horned guy at least did us a favour. That has to count for something.'

An hour later, they came to a dead end. Two stone doors stood facing each other. On each was carved an identical face, both covered in lichen and cobwebs. As they approached, two pairs of stone eyes slowly opened and regarded them coldly.

'One lies,' Jack said. 'The other tells only the truth.'

'So how do we work out the safe door?'

'We ask the right question.'

'But they will both give the same answer,' Corriwen protested. 'If you ask which way is safe, each will claim that it is their door.'

'That's the test,' Jack said, gloomily. He had been thinking about this as they walked, and had so far failed to come up with an answer. 'It's just another riddle.'

'One lies and the other speaks true,' Rionna said, almost whispering. 'But that is their weakness too.'

'How so?'

'Each knows what the other will say, whether true or false. And therefore each will give the same answer to only one question. And that answer will be wrong.'

She planted Megrin's staff down between her toes and faced the left-hand door. When she spoke, her voice was clear and sure.

'If I ask your brother which door leads to fire, what would he say?'

The stone eyes looked at her. The features began to twist and writhe with a rough, grinding sound. The mouth opened slowly and a gravelly voice replied.

'He would say my doorway leads there-to.'

'Then we choose your door too,' Rionna said before anyone could stop her. Kerry's breath drew in sharply.

For a long moment there was silence, then, a puff of

dust trickled out from a crack in the wall which gradually widened as they watched.

The door opened and a chilling blast of air almost took their breath away.

'No flames,' Kerry said, letting his breath out slowly. 'But I still don't get it. How did you know?'

'No matter which brother you ask the answer would still be the same.'

'It's going to take me forever to work that one out,' Kerry admitted.

Together they walked through the portal. It swung shut behind them with a heavy, final thud.

TWENTY FIVE

Overhead, the sky was an unearthly red and the landscape brown and parched. It stretched into the far distance. As far as Jack could see, nothing living grew here.

They stood together, the door of the cave closed behind them, and looked across miles of scorched earth, littered with craters and bare rocks which jutted up like stumps of old teeth.

'Any idea where we are?' Kerry asked, not expecting an answer.

Jack scanned the barren lands and all he saw was desolation. He wondered if his father had made the journey to this awful place before them.

Could he have survived here for so long?

As that thought struck him, Jack wondered if the four

of them could survive here at all. They had made it thus far, through everything that the nightshades and Bodron's spellbinding could throw at them. Yet this lifeless place looked as if it could swallow them up and leave no trace. He closed his eyes, weary and beset by doubt. Kerry and Corriwen would look to him for guidance and he could think of nothing except finding a way home, if there *was* a way home.

Corriwen touched him on the shoulder and he turned to her.

'I can see something up ahead,' she said, pointing. Jack stood close to follow her hand. Far out, where the seared land met the red sky, there was a faint smudge of darkness. It could have been a hill, or a storm or a cloud, but there was nothing to gauge distance by.

Kerry bent down to open his pack. He pulled out his water canteen and took a sip, then passed it around and they all drank gratefully.

He began to lay out his weapons: the short-sword, the old sling the Major had given him, and the bolas with its three weights that Connor had shown him how to use. Corriwen sat beside him and stropped her blades on her leather belt.

'I think we've run out of luck,' Kerry said flatly. 'The book said there was no way home.'

Corriwen interjected: 'Maybe it's wrong this time.'

'Maybe your father was here,' Kerry said softly. 'And maybe he just didn't . . .'

Kerry didn't say the word, but everybody knew what he meant.

The heartstone pulsed very gently. Jack's fingers closed around it and its slow beat somehow ignited a spark of hope within him. The Journeyman's stone still had some power here, maybe something to tell him. Jack suddenly thought that if he truly believed his father was dead, then this had all been for nothing, all the dangers and all the fear. He did not want to think he had led his friends through all that for no reason.

And he did not really want to consider the possibility that after battling through Temair and Eirinn and now Uaine, that there hadn't been a real purpose in all their travels.

Hadn't the Sky Queen spoken to him on Tara Hill? She had told him to find the gateway into summer and he had done so, to find himself in Uaine.

Everything they had done, every turn, every battle, had led them here.

There are no coincidences, he told himself. *No coincidences.*

There *must* be a purpose. If his father had found his way to this dreadful place, then Jack Flint would find him. And then, no matter what it took, he would help his friends find their way home.

Jack took out the *Book of Ways* and laid it on a dry flat stone. They watched as it opened its pages and flicked through almost to the very end. Jack thought for a second it would just snap shut, but it stopped at the final page.

An omen, he thought. We are near the end.

When the words finally appeared, they were red as the sky, red as blood.

For Journeyman the End of Ways
To stand at brink of the End of Days
The foulest foe lies here await
And traveller meets final fate
In darkest place, whence none return
Yet one is four and four is one
Light and life may still be won

Heart and soul may ever quail
Four as one may yet prevail
Prepare to meet the evil bane
That dwells on terror, fear and pain
Hold hard to faith in mortal fight
As dark prepares to smother light
And plunge all worlds to deepest night.

'Well, there's no mistaking that,' Kerry said, running a finger up his sword-blade. 'And I get the four-is-one bit. One for all and each for everybody else, right?'

'It's ever thus,' Corriwen agreed solemnly.

'At least it says there's a chance,' Jack said. That flicker of hope flared brighter. 'Light and life may still be won.'

'Except for the evil bane part,' Kerry said. He looked at the short-sword. 'I wish we had something better. Like a tommy-gun or a tank. Or one of those Apache helicoppers from the movies.'

Rionna and Corriwen looked at him blankly. Jack forced a wry grin. He patted the hilt of the broadsword.

'We'll have to make do with what we've got,' he said. 'Come on, let's go.'

A desert wind scoured and dust-devils spun towards them, ripping at their skin, shrieking like demons as they passed. Jack led them on, trudging mile after mile until they reached a tall rock outcrop.

Corriwen walked round the rock. It was taller than they were, and worn from years of wind-blown sand. On its lee side, old lichens formed a thin, dry skin.

'This looks like a statue,' she observed.

It did look like an old statue. Like a kneeling man, head bowed. But it was so worn there were no features, just a vague shape.

'It's just a shape cut by the wind,' Jack said. 'It'll wear it away to nothing eventually.'

A few hundred yards further, another stone stood out on the sand.

'That's definitely a statue,' Kerry said, pointing up at it. 'Look, you can make out the eyes and nose.'

It towered over them, broad and solid. It was clearly the carved figure of a man, standing with feet apart and arms by his sides. His face was tilted upwards and the mouth opened in an eternal, silent cry.

'Who'd put statues out here?' Kerry asked. 'That guy looks as if he's been blasted between the eyes.'

It was worn and cracked, corroded by the wind, but

unmistakeably a human. The figure looked as if he was in perpetual agony. Jack was glad when it was behind them and they walked forward, guided by the steady beat of the heartstone. The further they walked, the stronger came a smell of burning and hot stone, and with each step, Jack felt a sense of oppression settle heavier on him.

Beyond the sand, the ground became bare rock, riven with cracks. Tremors shuddered under their feet and pieces of stone shaled off to fall in noisy avalanches. Misshapen creatures clambered in and out of the fissures and gaped hungrily at them, but came no closer.

When they reached another statue, exhausted and footsore, Kerry fetched the canteen and they all drank gratefully. This figure was less eroded than the last, as if it had been carved more recently. The man was down on one knee, head bowed, resting his weight on a wide-bladed sword. He looked every inch the warrior. But for the worn stony surface, he looked as if he might wake, get to his feet and do battle.

'Looks like a tough guy,' Kerry said.

'He reminds me of my brother,' Corriwen said. 'He was a fine warrior.'

Kerry screwed the lid back on the canteen. 'That's the water half-done. We won't get much further.'

Jack looked ahead. The dark smudge on the horizon was noticeably closer, but in the hot, dry air, its shape wavered like a mirage and he couldn't tell whether it was a hill or a distant mountain. As they got closer it began to look ominously like the Black Tomb in Temair where Mandrake had raised the Morrigan and her terrible power from eons of sleep.

Corriwen shaded her eyes and stared at it sombrely, lips pursed. Jack understood how she felt. Neither she nor Kerry nor he would ever forget the nightmare time they'd spent within the Morrigan's lair. He put his arm around her shoulder and drew her attention. Corriwen tried to smile, but there was nothing much to smile about.

A final statue stood out like a sentinel. When they reached it, they stopped and looked up at the tall figure. This last one could have been carved only yesterday. Every detail of the man was etched with such craftsmanship that even the weave of his cloak and tunic were clear to see. He stood with one hand held high. In the other he grasped a long, jagged spear.

Jack looked at the statue's face, strong and handsome, with a short beard and hair held back by a braided band. Its stone eyes stared ahead blindly. He looked at the spear and his heart did a double-thump.

Hedda, the Scatha warrior woman of Eirinn had wielded a great spear she called the *Gae-bolg*, a deadly weapon with vicious barbs raking forward like thorns. This was an exact replica. He stepped nearer, marvelling at the similarity.

'It's Hedda's spear,' Kerry said. 'Exactly the same, even down to the spikes.'

'It's an awful weapon,' Rionna said. She reached out to touch it and as she did, Megrin's staff flared with electric blue light. Jack felt the heartstone vibrate and the great sword trembled in his hand. He moved to pull Rionna back, but she turned unexpectedly and his fingers touched the stone hand that wielded the spear.

The heartstone flashed. A spark leapt between his fingers and the statue's hand. It seared through every nerve of his body. White light exploded behind his eyes.

Jack staggered backwards, buckling at the knees. Kerry caught him before he fell.

'*Jeez*, Jack, what happened?'

The ground shuddered. Out on the plain, thin cracks opened in crazy zig-zags. In the far distance, thunder rolled across the sky and lightning forked upwards.

As Jack's vision began to clear, Kerry was yelling something in his ear. For a few moments he didn't know where he was. The heartstone was thrumming hard. The great sword felt as though it was trying to leap out of the scabbard.

A crack like a gunshot rang out and Corriwen let out a cry. Jack felt Kerry haul him backwards.

'It's going to fall,' he bawled, pointing at the statue.

Another crack rent the air, and another, and then a whole fusillade of them.

'Watch out!' Corriwen grabbed the back of his tunic and she and Kerry dragged Jack back.

'What's happening?'

There was a pop in his ears and sound came back with great clarity.

And then the statue moved.

The raised arm flexed. Pieces of stone broke off. The mouth opened in a snarl. The spear swung forward. Shards flew off in all directions.

The man-shape took a step forward. It swayed and shook its head. Then the grey stone began to change colour in a terrifying transformation.

Jack saw the weave of the cloak fold and sway, turning from solid stone to a green fabric. The grey hand opened and closed and became flesh-coloured.

'It's *alive,*' Rionna cried. Blue light was flickering up and down the length of Megrin's staff. At the sound of Rionna's voice, the living statue turned towards her. Its beard was now jet black and the hair dark and streaked with grey. But the eyes, though they were wide open, remained the colour of polished stone.

The statue let out a low cry and swung the spear towards them. Jack swept Rionna out of the path of the savage point.

The figure spun again, stabbing blindly and the spear-point slashed through the hood of Kerry's tunic as if it were paper. Kerry yelped, dodged away, fell over his back-pack and sprawled on the stony ground.

Jack dashed forward and slammed the spear down with the sword. Another jolt of power sizzled up the blade and into his arm with such a shock he almost dropped it. The blind fighter stalled. Kerry found his feet, the bolas in his hand, the three stones whirling on their strings. He threw it and the weights wrapped the strings round their opponent's legs.

The moving statue bellowed again, a great cry echoing over the barren plain, as it tried to take a step and fell headlong with an almighty crash. But still it managed to kick out, almost catching Corriwen on the side of the head, and quickly freed its legs from the entanglement. It was back on its feet in a flash.

'To hell with this,' Kerry yelled. 'It can't even see us.'

With that, he bent and scooped up a stone, slotted it into his sling and let fly. The rock caught the man on the back of the head. He went down on one knee, shook his head violently. Jack saw two small objects spin away.

The statue turned and when he did, his eyes were open and they were piercing blue. The eyes found his and their gazes locked. A line of blood trickled down the man's cheek.

'Who are you?' he asked, in a Scottish accent almost exactly like the Major's. 'And what in all the worlds are you doing with *my* sword?'

TWENTY SIX

'It's *my* sword,' Jack asserted. The mysterious shock of power still tingled up and down his arm. The warrior was tall and broad-shouldered, arms taut with muscle, and scarred from many a fight. There was something strangely familiar about him.

The man's blue eyes held him fast.

'You stole it, lad. How you did it and how you came to be in this place, I don't know. But I'll have it back now.'

'Yeah, right,' Kerry sneered. 'It's four to one, and we've beaten worse than you. Many a time.'

'I must be dreaming this,' the big man said. His free hand went to his forehead and he swayed a little. 'You're imps. Changelings.'

'We're not,' Jack countered. Corriwen had moved to the

side in a flanking motion. Kerry's sword was at the ready. 'We're real. But I'm not sure *you* are.'

'Your speech is familiar. Where are you from and how did you get here?'

'We're from very far away,' Kerry butted in. 'And we're on a mission. So just let us pass and we'll be on our way.'

The man's eyes flicked from Kerry to Corriwen and back to Jack.

'That *is* my sword. There's only one other like it.'

'We know that,' Corriwen said. 'The other one's mine.'

The man kept staring, measuring Jack with his eyes. Then he saw the amberhorn bow slung on Jack's shoulder.

'And where did you get that bow? It's not the work of anyone in Uaine.'

He looked at Rionna. 'And you, girl. I've seen that staff before. It belongs to a friend of mine. How did you come by it?'

Jack held a hand up, playing for time. Sudden, unexpected emotions were churning inside him. 'Hold on. One minute ago you were a statue and now *you're* asking all the questions.'

The man froze. His blue eyes were fixed below Jack's chin. The spear-point was suddenly at Jack's throat where his tunic opened. Jack hadn't even seen it move.

The man's face was slack with shock or surprise. He looked as if he'd been kicked.

'The stone. On the chain. How did you come by it?'

He jabbed the spear and Jack could feel the sharp point digging into his skin.

'Just who are you? *What* are you?'

'My name is Jack Flint.'

'And he's the Journeyman,' Kerry added. 'Appointed by the Sky Queen to fight her battles, so just you watch out.'

The spear dropped to the ground. The man let out a groan and sank to his knees as if all the strength had drained from him. Now his face was a picture of anguish.

'Jack ... *Jack* ...'

Tears sprung to the man's blue eyes and spilled freely down his cheeks. In that moment Jack *knew*. His heart felt as if it was about to burst.

'Oh ... oh, my ... how many years?'

'He's fourteen,' Kerry piped up. 'Same as me.'

'Fourteen years ... Jack ...' The man's voice choked. 'You don't know me. Couldn't know me.'

Corriwen and Kerry gaped in astonishment as realisation dawned on them. Their eyes turned to Jack and they saw his eyes sparkle, his expression rapt.

'I think I do,' Jack whispered.

'I am Jonathan Cullian Flint. I put that heartstone around your neck and carried you through the Homeward Gate to safety. It seems like only yesterday.'

He closed his eyes. 'Fourteen years! Fourteen *lost* years.'

Tears streamed down Jack's cheeks. Jonathan Cullian Flint reached out to him and Jack walked into his father's tight embrace.

TWENTY SEVEN

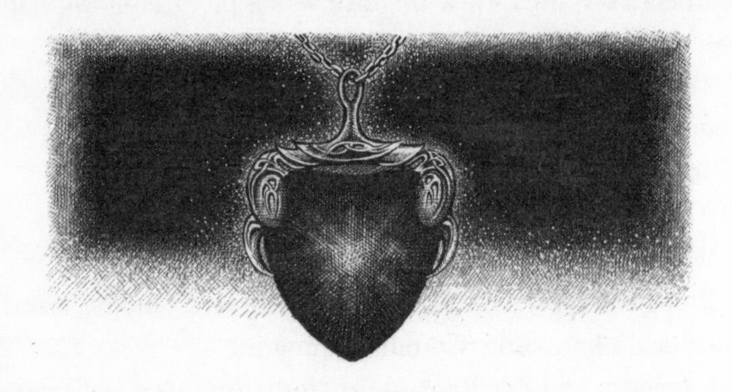

Jack could hardly believe he had found his father. He still couldn't quite believe that the statue on the red plain had moved, begun to fight and become human. Not just any human, the man he had dreamed of finding for so long. It was too much to take in.

As Jonathan Flint led them towards a rocky crevasse to shelter, Jack couldn't keep his eyes off the man he barely knew, but had loved with fierce pride since childhood. Now he was confused and uncertain of what to say, what to ask.

A thousand questions crowded his mind. Where had he been? Why had he abandoned Jack in the ring of standing stones as a baby? What had happened to his mother?

Jonathan Flint moved stiffly, as if he hadn't used his

muscles in a long time. Jack took in his tall frame, the scars on his strong arms and the dark hair which fell over the brow, so like his own.

He had always tried to picture his father, but the image was never distinct. He had no memory of his face, just a hazy recollection of strength and protection. He had never imagined him as a cloaked and armed warrior.

By the time they reached the shelter, the shock and emotion had overwhelmed Jack and he sank down, utterly exhausted. His father leant back against the rock and closed his eyes for a moment. Corriwen, Kerry and Rionna stood uncertainly close by, not wishing to intrude, but after a moment Jonathan Flint opened his eyes again. He took Jack's hand in his, cupping it tightly as if to reassure himself that the hand was real, then beckoned the others forward and asked their names.

'Corriwen Redthorn, Kerrigan Malone, Rionna Willow. I don't know you, not yet, but I can see you are friends of my son, and my guess is you've followed a hard road at his side. For that, I thank you from the bottom of my heart.'

He squeezed Jack's hand again and, motioning the others to sit, turned to his son and said: 'Forgive me for losing your childhood.'

Jack tried to speak, but his father held up his free hand to hush him.

'But it was a desperate time,' Jack's father said. 'A truly desperate time, and I wanted you to live, no matter the cost.'

'We came to Uaine because of all the worlds of men, it was the most beautiful. The Copperplate binding spell had brought lasting harmony for generations. We made a home where we could watch the sunrise and sunset and hear the waves on the shore. As beautiful a place as ever there was.

'Just after you were born, Jack, Bodron gathered the Copperplates, Uaine's talismans. He brought the spells together and found ways to change them, hoping to gain the secrets of their power. Yet power can be used for good or evil, and the greater the power, the greater the evil.

'Bodron corrupted the great spells and he summoned up a Shadowlord. Perhaps he thought his summoning would give him power over it and he could make it his creature. But Bodron was wrong. The Shadowlord had the greater power, Bodron became its puppet, spreading fear and nightmare across this world.

'That was when the Geasan summoned me to ask for my help. But when I was at their council, the nightshades came in their hordes and I discovered the Shadowlord's true purpose. It wanted the heartstone keys, and sent its nightshades to search for them.

'When I returned home your mother was gone, taken by the Shadowlord's minions.

'But despite the peril she found herself in, alone with her baby, she had kept you safe. She hid you in a secret place beyond the nightshades' reach.

'It was then that I knew I had to get you, and the heartstone, to safety, because my next quest was to find your mother. If the Shadowlord had her, then it also had the white heartstone, the twin of the one you wear on your neck. With both, its power would be vast, and irresistible and I could not risk that.

'They pursued us all the way to the Homeward Gate, and only luck and the Sky Queen's protection got me to Cromwath Blackwood. I put the heart around your neck because I knew it would be safe with the Major, at least for a while.

'I promised you I would come back for you. It was the only promise I ever made that I never kept.

'But I promise you this. If she is still alive, I will find your mother and bring her out of this evil place.'

For a long time there was silence while Jack took in his father's story. Back in her wildwood, Megrin had mentioned his mother. Since the Major could tell him nothing of her, Jack had assumed she was dead.

Now he had found his father and discovered that he had a mother who might still be alive. It was almost too much to take in at one time.

Kerry, Corriwen and Rionna had listened eagerly to the tale. Later, when they had fallen into an exhausted sleep, huddled together in the crevice, Jonathan Flint drew Jack closer to share his warmth.

'The Major never told me anything,' Jack finally said. 'He said I had to wait until I was older.'

'That's as it should be,' Jonathan Flint agreed. 'The secrets of the worlds and the gateways must be guarded at all costs. I discovered them by accident when I was just a boy of your age. My friend Tom Lynn and I explored Cromwath Blackwood and found the ring of stones. Tom stepped through and vanished. I searched for him for a long time in some strange places.'

'So that story is real? Tom Lynn came back ten years later, and he hadn't aged a day. But his mind was gone, so people said.'

'There are some terrible places beyond the gates. Places where madness and terror reign. I have been to some. I was luckier, because in all my travels, I was being led towards the heartstone and the *Book of Ways* which allowed me to find my way back to the Homeward Gate, and I also learned that the heartstone and the book were created in the dawn of time to let the Journeyman open the ways to all the worlds.

'I learned this from the Great Dagda after I helped him save Eirinn from the Morrigan's sea-ogres. That was when I met your mother, the Lady Lauralen. She is the daughter of the Dagda and the Sky Queen, and she loved me enough to stay by my side in the mortal worlds.'

'That's why the lady said it,' Jack said, remembering the magical meeting with the Sky Queen on Tara Hill. 'Heart of my heart, she told me.'

'That's because you are. Blood of her blood. And she

has been guiding you. She is all that is good, in the constant fight against all that is evil.'

Jack told his father everything of his childhood in the Major's old house and his long friendship with Kerry Malone, days at school and fishing with Kerry in the streams. He told of that Halloween night when the moving darkness had engulfed the Major's house and how the old man had kept it at bay while they escaped down the stairs to the secret passageway and found themselves hunted through Cromwath Blackwood.

Jonathan Flint listened intently as Jack recounted their adventures in Temair and Eirinn, and then their journey with Megrin to Bodron's Keep.

'It was the book that saved us,' Jack said. 'It swallowed the Copperplates. We fought Bodron, all four of us, and Megrin too. Then everything went crazy and we slid into the pit and here we are.'

Jack paused, thinking for a moment. Then he took the heartstone from his neck, drew out the great sword and offered both to his father.

'These belong to the Journeyman,' he said. 'You take them.'

Jonathan Flint was choked with emotion.

'No, Jack. My time is done. I have been in these Shadowlands too long. You have earned the sword and the name.

'The Great Dark Lord, the master of all Shadowlords, reigns supreme here and I have fought him many times in all his guises. The last I remember, he showed me his true shape and turned his eyes on me and I felt my blood turn to stone. Since then, nothing. Until something unfroze me and I could move again.'

'It was the heartstone,' Jack said. 'The Journeyman's heart.'

'It's *your* heart, Journeyman.'

TWENTY EIGHT

The Dark Tower reached into the red sky. It stood, bleak as a tombstone. The closer they got, the more the heartstone shuddered. With every step, Jack was overwhelmed by a feeling of oppression.

'It is waiting,' Jonathan Flint said. 'It knows the heartstone is near.'

'Then maybe we should take it as far away from here as we can,' Kerry said.

'No,' Jack countered. 'The book said we had a chance to defeat it. "With staff, book and heart, prevail." We've faced so much, we can't give up now.'

His father gave him a measuring look, pride shining in his eyes. 'Perhaps not much of a chance,' he said. 'But a chance all the same. Remember those petrified heroes, turned to stone by its dead eyes, long ago. As I was. I fought it and beat it back, again and again, and each time it came out to do battle it was stronger. It has the strength of all the souls it has stolen. It will use everything it has against us.'

When they finally reached the great bastion, standing in its shadow, Jack saw that the walls were not as featureless as they had appeared. Their surface was intricately carved with thousands of human skulls, row upon row, blindly leering at all who approached.

Kerry stretched out his hand to touch one of the carvings and then jerked back with a cry of alarm as the skull's gaping mouth suddenly snapped shut.

'I can feel its foulness,' Corriwen said. 'Like death. Like disease.'

'There's no way in,' Jack said, scanning the walls.

'Good,' Kerry muttered. 'Whatever's in there should stay there.'

'We must find a way,' Jonathan Flint said. He strode towards the wall, and stabbed his long spear into a hanging jaw. The skull rolled out onto the ground at their feet.

For a moment nothing moved and then, without warning, that part of the wall collapsed in a roar of skull grinding on skull. Jonathan Flint turned fast and swept them away from an avalanche of bone.

A white dust took several minutes to clear. Corriwen and Rionna kept their arms over their mouths and noses so as not to breathe any of it in. Before them was a gap that cut through the skull wall.

'I think a way has been opened for us,' Jack's father said.

He turned to look at them all. 'I have to go in there, but you should wait here.'

Jack shook his head, though his heart was pounding. 'No. If you're going, so am I. We've come this far.'

Kerry stood with him, shoulder to shoulder.

'And I go with Jack,' he said. 'Always have, always will.'

'And I too,' Corriwen declared. Rionna said nothing. She held tight to Corriwen's hand and nodded silently.

Jonathan Flint took in a slow breath, turned back, and stepped through the gap in the wall.

The place reeked of rot and decay. Jack thought he could hear a low moaning, the sound of a thousand people in despair, but they walked on. Jonathan Flint led the way, with the great spear on his shoulder, ready for battle. Kerry had loaded his sling and held the short-sword in one hand.

Four is one ... Jack repeated the words from the book to himself. *And now five.* They had to stay together, because whatever waited for them, waited with foul intent. And it wouldn't wait long.

Jack concentrated his thoughts on his mother. 'Please let her be alive,' he whispered.

His father clamped a hand on his shoulder. Despite his fear, despite the apprehension that clenched his stomach, his father's touch gave him strength.

'You have grown to be the man I always hoped you'd be,' Jonathan Flint said in a soft voice. 'If I don't get the chance later, you should know that now.'

Jack nodded, but he was too tense, too scared, to feel anything at all.

The path opened into a vast amphitheatre, surrounded by a maze of passages. In the centre of this arena, a dark mound rose like an ancient tomb. Red light flickered, the only illumination. Rasping whispers clamoured in Jack's head, in words he could not understand, but he sensed malign intent. Corriwen clamped her hands to her ears to block out the voices, but to no avail.

Jack followed close behind his father, as they worked their way towards the centre of the amphitheatre, with Kerry at his shoulder, keeping Corriwen and Rionna behind them.

The sound of voices increased with every step and troubling images flickered across Jack's consciousness: images of blood and death; of shadowy things grinning from corners; of dark beasts hunched and turning to fix him with dreadful eyes.

Kerry shuddered. 'I'm getting awful nightmares. I think I'm going mad.'

'It is toying with us,' Jack's father said. 'Wearing us down.'

Corriwen clapped her hands to her eyes. 'Get out of my mind ... get *out* of me!'

When she took her hands away, her cheeks were streaked with tears. Rionna put her arm around her shoulders. To Kerry, she seemed the least affected, and he knew it was because she had spent her life protecting herself from those evil forces.

The black mound hunched in the distance as they walked into the open.

Suddenly, without warning, three hooded shapes came out of nowhere, shrieking.

Nightshades. In an instant Jack was back at the Major's house while the darkness flowed through the rooms like a disease. *Shadowmasters.*

Jack felt their numbing cold as he leapt to the side, instinctively swinging his sword. He glimpsed a wavering shape that seemed almost insubstantial, and within it, a skeletal face.

'Don't let them touch you!' The nightshades had touched him when he first fled through the ringstones, a foul contagion that had had to be burned out of his flesh.

Jonathan Flint's spear jabbed, once, twice, fast strikes. The spectre screamed and when Jack's father pulled the spearpoint out, it folded in upon itself, disintegrating to fluttering scraps.

Kerry and Corriwen were twisting and turning, Kerry hitting where he could and Corriwen trying to strike with a deadly arrow. The spectres were fast, but the pair were faster, keeping just out of reach.

Corriwen drew Jack's bow and aimed. The arrow caught the nightshade in its middle, slowing it down just enough for Kerry to slash down with the short-sword. Sparks ran up and down his blade and he cried out in pain. Jonathan Flint stepped in and slammed his spear deep within the writhing figure. He pinned it to the ground, savagely twisting the weapon until it stopped moving.

The third nightshade came screeching towards Rionna. She raised Megrin's staff and a jolt of blue light stopped the creature in mid-flight. Jack stepped past her and lashed out with the great sword. When the blade sliced, he felt a shock run up his arm, and an icy sensation of deep cold. He pulled the blade out and the nightshade imploded with a hiss.

As they stood together, breathing hard, the shrouded figures on the ground crumpled into tatters that swirled around as if stirred by a wind and then drifted away.

This is just the start, Jack thought to himself.

His father turned to him. 'It was too easy. They were here to hold us up.'

Jack nodded. It *had* been just the start. Before he could say anything, Kerry cocked his head.

'Something's coming.'

'I hear it,' Corriwen said. She looked around wildly.

They all drew together, trying vainly to hear where it was coming from. It got louder with every second.

At first, Jack thought he could see grey shadow sweeping across the tangle of passageways. The heartstone throbbed powerfully on his chest. Jonathan Flint raised his arm protectively to push them behind him.

Then Jack realised it was no shadow, but a tide of creatures leaping and clambering along the walls of the maze, like a swarm of rats, but much bigger, and faster.

'I don't like this,' Kerry muttered, reaching again for his sword. 'There's millions of them.'

Creatures came streaming from all around. They were all shapes and sizes. Some had great pale eyes and some no eyes at all, or mouths in the middle of thin chests. Some had scales and others had slimy, oozing skin. But they all had one purpose and that was to destroy the five people who stood facing them.

Jack held his sword steady. His free hand clutched the heartstone and as he touched it a clear voice spoke, deep inside his head.

Heart of my heart, soul of my soul.

The words of the Sky Queen rang in his mind. His heart thudded. This voice was clear and gentle, like the Sky Queen's, but different. He opened his fingers and stared at the heartstone. It rippled with light. Vibrant colours spangled under its polished surface. Despite the approaching wave of horrors, he couldn't draw his eyes away. The light held him.

Corriwen was saying something to him, but he barely heard her. The sound of the advancing creatures had faded to the background. Colours flashed in front of his eyes and in their midst a face began to form.

It was a heart-shaped, slender face with long, spun-gold hair. As majestic as the Sky Queen had been on Tara Hill, but younger.

You have returned. My Journeyman. The voice came from deep inside him.

She was beautiful.

Her eyes were closed, as if she was in a deep sleep, but her voice, clear as crystal, tugged at him. In that instant he knew that this was his mother.

With a great effort, he dragged his attention away from the vision. The repulsive swarm of contorted creatures was still pouring towards them, shrieking and hissing. Jonathan Flint stalked forward to meet them, spear at the ready. Jack ran after him and grabbed his wrist.

'She called me!'

His father stopped in his tracks. His attention had been fixed on the advancing horde, but he turned to his son. Jack gripped him tight.

'My mother. She *called* me. I'm going to find her.'

Before Jonathan Flint could reply, Jack pressed the great sword into his free hand.

'Stay alive,' he begged. 'I *will* find her. For us.'

Jack spun on his heel, not waiting for his father's reaction or to risk him holding him back. He hurried towards his friends. Corriwen and Kerry were tense and ready to fight. Rionna watched the three of them, lit by the soft glow from Megrin's staff.

'I have to go,' Jack told them. 'Watch his back. Don't let them get him, not now.'

'You can't leave us now,' Kerry protested. 'Where are you going?'

'My mother,' Jack said. 'She's alive.'

'How do you know?' Corriwen asked, her eyes fixed on the advancing monsters.

Jack raised the heart. 'She spoke to me. I *saw* her.'

'Then go,' Corriwen said resolutely. 'Find her. End your quest.'

Kerry agreed. 'Yeah, Jack. Don't you worry,' he said, with more bravado than certainty. His voice was shaky. 'The things under my bed were ten times worse. We'll maulicate these boogers.'

'We stand here,' Corriwen said very seriously. 'Friends to the end.'

Jack hugged them both hard and stepped towards Rionna who had Megrin's staff braced in both hands.

'I need light,' he said. Rionna closed her eyes. He heard her pure musical note and the staff suddenly blazed with blue fire. Rionna offered the staff to Jack and he took it in his hand and walked determinedly towards the squat stone mound in the centre of the amphitheatre, clutching the heartstone in his other hand.

As he touched it, the wall dissolved under his fingers, shrinking from his warmth. He stepped forward and time seemed to stop. Behind him the cacophony of the approaching creatures slowed to a deep rumble and faded to silence. All Jack could hear was the beat of his own heart. For a few seconds he was in total darkness, then Megrin's light flared bright, illuminating a small circle around him.

TWENTY NINE

There was danger here, and it was all around. Jack could feel it. Foul images of death and destruction came to him again: bloody battlefields, carrion roaks, mouldering skeletons, all the horrors that had been or might still be to come.

Get out. Get OUT.

A command inside his head sent him reeling. Another image began to form in his mind.

He saw his father with Kerry and Corriwen at his side as a vast army of monstrosities overwhelmed them, biting and ripping and tearing.

Get out, the foul voice screamed. *There is nothing for you here. Run! Save them!*

Jack couldn't tell whether the voice was real or an illusion, but he fought against it. He closed his eyes and forced himself to picture his own thoughts; his friendship with Kerry; the day they saved Corriwen; the touch of his father's hand; the warmth of his mother's voice. It took a great effort of will, but these clean and pure memories began to overcome the foul invasion and the horrific images began to fade.

Over and above the cold whisperings, he could hear something else, and it sounded like the beat of another human heart.

Jack held Megrin's staff high. Gauzy shapes moved around him, now silent as moths and barely visible. Jack sensed their hatred, but he continued into the darkness until a glimmer of light began to glow ahead of him.

Megrin's light grew stronger and Jack felt the atmosphere change. The ground trembled, but he kept his grip on the heartstone as he edged forward.

In front of him, the silvery light grew in intensity. Tangles of moving darkness surrounded it in coils, but as Jack approached, the glow strengthened.

Then Jack saw her.

His heart leapt into his throat and left him feeling breathless and dizzy. At first he thought it was just a floating illumination, but as he stepped nearer it began to take form. It was a woman, still as death, wrapped in a cocoon of sparkling light.

She was pale, as if carved from marble. She floated, suspended within the light, which played on her delicate features, and made her long fair hair gleam. Both hands were crossed over her chest and at her throat pulsed another heartstone, cut and polished just like the one Jack held, but this one clear as a diamond and aglow with white light.

Jack felt as if his heart would burst.

Heart of my heart. The gentle voice spoke within him again. *Soul of my soul.*

Jack gripped the heartstone. It beat steadily, matching the pulse of the crystal heart. His feet moved of their own accord and brought him closer.

You come at last ...

He heard the words, and felt the joy in them. It matched the joy that swelled inside his own chest.

To bring me back ...

He leant towards his mother. Silver light tinkled as if the dust in the air were charged with power. He took her hands in his. They were cold as stone and there was no sign of life.

Some compulsion made him lean further until he was only inches away from her perfect face.

And the two heartstones touched.

Light blazed so brightly that he felt it sear through every nerve in his body. In that moment Jack was overwhelmed by a flood of images and memories as the white radiance sizzled through every nerve.

He saw his mother and father walking on a beach towards the rising sun. He saw the dark shadow envelop their home and he watched the final, desperate battle with the nightshades. He saw his father lift him from a cradle and fight his way out, while a great pit opened, taking his mother into darkness.

He heard the mad screeches of the things that hunted

them through woodland until they reached the stone gate. He felt again the *twist* as his father stepped through. He heard him blow on his horn and wrap him tight, with the heartstone and the *Book of Ways* secured in the blanket.

The memories streamed through his mind, surging with colour and images, flooding him with knowledge of his mother and father and their lives, and what had brought them both to this place where all roads ended.

In the brilliant radiance, a soft hand cupped his face. She stood before him, tall and slender. Wide blue eyes regarded him and in them he saw infinite wisdom. Tears coursed down her sculpted cheeks. Her hands slid around his shoulders and brought him into her warmth.

'My baby,' she said, through her tears. 'My boy. My Journeyman.'

He moved into her embrace and the two heartstones came together again. All around them, the prison which had held her for so long disintegrated under their combined power.

They stood together, mother and son, each holding tight to the other, while their surroundings crumbled to dust and blew away.

Jack's mother closed her eyes. She whispered softly and the blazing light slowly faded and Jack saw they were back in the middle of the amphitheatre.

His father stood tall with the great sword. Kerry, Corriwen and Rionna were behind him.

And the hordes of the obscene, misshapen creatures that had hunched and lurched towards them were still as statues, frozen in a moment of time.

Jack heard a ringing in his ears, and suddenly sound and movement returned and he could hear the growling and chittering of the grotesque army as it approached.

THIRTY

'It begins,' his mother said, in barely more than a whisper. 'And it ends here.'

As if she had called out to him, Jack's father turned towards them. Their eyes met and held. Neither his mother nor father spoke, but Jack saw the love and regret in his father's gaze.

He mouthed one word that was swallowed in the noise from the tide of grotesque creatures surging across the arena.

Lauralen.

Jonathan Flint looked at his son and nodded slowly, just once. In that small gesture he managed to convey so much. Jack knew his father was thanking him for bringing Lauralen Flint back. And he sensed the powerful bond that he had dreamed of since childhood. For the second time that day Jack's heart felt as if it would burst.

Kerry turned and when he saw the fair-haired woman his eyes grew so wide they looked as if they might pop out.

'Wow!' It was all he could manage.

Corriwen just gazed at her as if Jack's mother was an apparition. Jack still wasn't sure she was not.

'The Great Lord of Darkness comes,' Lauralen said.

'First we have to fight these beasties,' Kerry finally found his tongue. Jack passed the glowing staff back to Rionna.

Jonathan Flint swept his gaze around them all.

'As we stand here,' he said, 'I wish it were different. But such is fate.' His voice was steady and calm.

'Always for the light,' said Lauralen, just as calmly. She showed no fear. 'Always for the right. It was ever thus.'

Jack's father turned to face the approaching creatures. As he swung the great sword Jack thought it fit his hand as if it were made for him.

The horde of sprites slowed their advance. For a moment, all Jack could hear was the scratching of claws on stony ground. Corriwen readied her bow. Kerry was muttering something to himself. It took Jack a moment to recognise it was the poem that he had helped him learn at school. It was about Robert the Bruce at the battle of Bannockburn.

Now's the day, and now's the hour; see the front o' battle lour . . .

Kerry had his short-sword in one hand and swung the heavy bolas in the other.

'Ready as I'm ever going to be,' he breathed. 'But I'd rather be fishing any day of the week.'

Lauralen Flint silently handed Megrin's staff to Rionna who gripped it tight.

Jack expected the creatures to come surging towards them at any moment, but they did not. Instead, they began to mill together, forming a tight pack.

'What are they doing?' Corriwen's voice was tight.

They clustered together, piling one on top of the other, forming a mound of arms and legs and claws and tails.

Jack's mother stood calmly. The heartstone gleamed at her neck, pulsing in time with the one Jack wore.

The heap of wriggling bodies began to change shape. All the hideous creatures merged together, sinking into each other until there was just a featureless shape in front of them.

'Is that it?' Kerry asked. 'Are they dead?'

As if in reply, the shape gave an enormous shudder. Jack watched in horror as it expanded, growing upwards into a pillar until it towered above them.

A huge head swelled upon massive shoulders. Its toes grew into curved claws, two upon each foot. Fingers stretched into long, hooked talons. Horns grew on its head, spiralling and ridged like a monstrous ram.

A mouth opened, showing row upon row of jagged black teeth and from it boomed a mighty, triumphant laugh that echoed madly around the walls of the amphitheatre.

Jonathan Flint turned to face it. Kerry looked at Jack, his eyes wide with apprehension. Corriwen had drawn the bow, ready to shoot. Rionna had raised Megrin's staff.

Jack realised with dismay that neither he nor his mother

were armed. They had nothing but the two heartstones. Jack felt his own heartstone beat harder.

The beast laughed again, and the ground heaved. It raised its arms and spread them out on either side. Flames burst into life and raced up and down its body, twisting around its arms and legs.

It swung a vast arm around and pointed a claw at Jonathan Flint. A bolt of fire exploded out. Jack's father disappeared in a gout of flame, and Jack cried out in alarm.

Then he saw him, twenty yards distant, unscathed.

Where he had stood, the rock was flowing white-hot. The reek of burning filled the air.

Jonathan Flint was moving fast.

His spear was at his shoulder. Jonathan Flint's back arched and he launched it straight at the fiery shape. Where it struck, tongues of flame billowed out and Jack saw the monster stagger.

It can be hurt, he thought.

Two clawed hands swung round and gripped the spear. Fire surged between the hands, but the great weapon did not burn. Grunting, it pulled the spear free. The puncture holes in its body spewed burning liquid and acrid fumes.

But Jonathan Flint was still moving, swinging the Scatha's sword in his right hand. Kerry and Corriwen, to Jack's amazement, were on his heels. He made to follow them, but his mother pressed on his shoulder.

'Wait,' she said softly, and that word carried an enormous weight of command. Jack froze. Lauralen Flint placed her free hand on Rionna's shoulder and together they stood, watching the deadly battle. Jack was desperate with the need to fight with his friends and at his father's side, but the hand on his shoulder made him stay.

He saw his father duck under a mighty arm as it came sweeping down. The sword flashed, slashed, and a huge claw tumbled away and landed with a thump, missing Kerry by a whisker.

Corriwen raised her bow. She was moving fast, a red-headed streak. One arrow shot out and stabbed between the jagged teeth. Foul steam billowed and it roared again.

It swung at her and a sizzling jolt traced her as she dashed away, scoring the ground in puffs of vapour.

Kerry jinked past the twitching claw. Without warning it flipped over and scuttled after him, a nightmare on four claws and a hooked thumb, moving with spider-like speed.

He let out a yell of fright and ran as the thing scrabbled after him, trailing blood that sizzled as it hit the ground. Corriwen launched another arrow, again high on the monster's body, just as Kerry blundered between its legs. Briefly distracted, it missed a slashing grab for him. Instinctively Kerry jabbed and the sword turned pink then flopped like a wilted leaf. A vast hoof raised over his head and stamped down again. For a second, Jack saw Kerry disappear in a cloud of fumes and then he was out the other side, ducking and rolling as it stamped again, so hard that the whole dark world trembled.

Jack watched with a mixture of fear and pride as his friends and his father fought the monstrosity. He wanted to run in and help them, to do *something* other than watch, but his mother's hand stayed firmly on his shoulder, and he found he could not leave her.

Corriwen launched another arrow and another, shooting and reloading fast. They spiked around its hideous face, but the beast brushed them away and came at her. She leapt aside and Jonathan Flint strode in again with the great sword. It blazed with light as he slashed, tearing huge gouges in the monster's thighs, gouges that formed mouths with jagged teeth that gnashed in fury.

Kerry found Jonathan Flint's spear. It looked much too big for him but he managed it nonetheless. He ran to his side, with the spear raised up. Jack's father stabbed hard and the beast faltered, giving Kerry the chance to put all his strength into one hard lunge.

It staggered, bellowing. Jack watched in amazement as it rocked back and then began to tumble forward. It happened as if in slow motion. Jonathan Flint grabbed Kerry's hood and hauled him back just as the behemoth toppled and hit the ground with enormous force.

'Is it dead?' Rionna asked.

'No,' Lauralen said. 'The great beast can never die, for he is not alive as we know it. He is the sum of all the evil he has gathered to himself.'

Now Jonathan Flint, Corriwen and Kerry were backing off. The beast was on all fours, scoring gouges in the ground. It seemed to curl into itself. The hand that had chased Kerry crawled towards it, clawed its way up and sank back into its warty skin.

Before their eyes, the arms and legs shrank back into the main body until all they could see was a twitching mass.

'It's changing again,' Rionna said.

'Stand by me,' Lauralen told Jack. 'Now we play our part. We have two heartstones and you have more power than you know. We will need all of it.'

Jack saw the surface of the mass rip wide open and what emerged made his stomach clench. At first it was a writhing mass of worms, wriggling and looping and slimy, like branched tentacles, except that each one ended in a head that was grotesquely human. It uncoiled, still swelling and the tentacles hardened into jointed limbs. The head, on a long, segmented neck, reminded Jack of a praying mantis.

A scraping voice spoke in Jack's head.

Lost forever, mortal. The voice was like rot and sickness. He felt it deep inside him and he shuddered. *Your pain will be eternal. I will burn you for all time and feast on your anguish.*

Jack clapped his hands to his head, staggering under the mental assault.

His mother laid a soft hand on his head and the sensation faded until he could open his eyes once more. The heartstones thrummed together in powerful harmony.

'Begone.' Her voice was clear. 'You will *never* have him.'

Give me what I will have. Give it now and he will suffer less. The Mailachan Mhor commands.

'You are no Great Lord,' she said. Jack could hear the words but couldn't see her lips move. 'You are the king of nothingness.'

I will bring perpetual night and pain. I will ravage! I will cover all in darkness.

The great wings whooped in the air. Its neck stretched

out towards them, head swelling and contorting, bent to the ground.

Jack watched in horror as a great eye began to open. He could see fire swirling under the scaly eyelid. His mother made no move.

Something thudded at Jack's side. His hand found the satchel. His other hand went to the heartstone and its throb rippled through him. His fingers opened the bag and touched the *Book of Ways*. Before he knew it, it was in his hand.

His mother reached and grasped Megrin's staff with one hand on top of Rionna's. In her other, she raised the crystal heartstone. Instinctively Jack imitated her. He held his own heartstone up before him. The book twisted in his hand.

His mother stepped in front of Rionna and the creature's eye turned to follow her. It was as red as boiling lava. Rocks burst asunder as it began to focus.

Jonathan Flint ran in, his sword raised. The eye swivelled towards him.

Suddenly Megrin's staff blazed with incandescent white light. A jolt of power blasted out from the monster's eye, a beam of darkness. Every nerve in Jack's body shrivelled, and intense cold shuddered through his bones.

Megrin's light met the creature's dark-light head on. Lauralen Flint held the staff in a firm grip, eyes wide, concentrating. The *Book of Ways* twisted again in Jack's hand. A strange, juddering sound came as the darkness tried to engulf Megrin's light.

Lauralen Flint held up her heartstone.

And Megrin's light winked out.

The monstrous beast roared in triumph.

Jack's heart lurched. But suddenly the *Book of Ways* opened in his numbed hand, just as the beast's glare blasted straight at his mother.

A blow struck the crystal heartstone with such force that the air about them seemed to rip to shreds.

The heartstone glowed. The deathly blast leapt from her stone to Jack's in a beam of blue. The heartstone turned the light yet again. A beam stabbed down and hit the open book. Pure copper on the page turned to gold and the dark-light, now a line of brilliant yellow was hurled back in the direction it had come.

It struck the beast right in the glaring eye.

Then the devil got a taste of his own. The light from the Copperplates melted the eye in its socket. The great beast juddered and its wings froze in mid-beat. Its foul head bent backwards and the mouth gaped like a cavern. A deep, hollow rumble rolled over them and then the mouth closed with a crash.

Jack's mother stood watching, heartstone in her hand.

The beast swayed on its horned feet, and Jack stared in fascination as its movement began to slow until it was almost still.

A sudden wind whipped up the sand around them, swirling around the monster. It gained strength, but they stood firm, holding on to one another as the creature swayed in the blast and then toppled backwards and crashed to the ground . . .

It shattered into a million fragments that crumbled to dust which was swept away by the gale. The wind died as quickly as it had begun and they stood, six of them together, in a land scoured clean.

All around them was emptiness, no rocks, no stone, no amphitheatre, nothing.

Jack's mother let out a long sigh and took his hand in hers.

Jonathan Flint came up beside them, wrapped his arms around both of them.

'You came back,' Lauralen said.

THIRTY ONE

'Find our way,' Lauralen Flint had asked. Rionna, still holding the staff, bent her head and began to sing, so softly that Jack could barely hear her. Kerry and Corriwen stood with them, not yet able to comprehend that it was all over.

Far out in the emptiness, a faint curve on the horizon showed a pale arch. Lauralen smiled.

'You have more in you than you could guess,' she told Rionna. 'Uaine will be glad of it in days to come.'

When they finally stood before the archway, Jack could see green fields on the far side, flowers and bright sunshine. The faint call of songbirds welcomed them.

Megrin stood alone. Behind her, all that remained of Bodron's Keep were a few mossy mounds, as if they had crumbled centuries ago.

Rionna stepped forward with the staff and offered it to her.

'Oh no, my dear,' Megrin said. 'It fits your hand better. A new generation brings new life to Uaine.'

Now Jack Flint knew who he was. He had stepped alone through the gateway to Uaine, but he was no longer alone. He had his mother and father, and he had the best friends anyone could wish for. His happiness could not have been more complete.

They had woken to a new dawn. Dew was like diamonds on the grass. His mother roused him with a touch on his cheek, took him by the hand and led him through the morning glades, to a small forest lake. A gentle mist floated over the surface and nothing stirred.

They sat by the water in silence, not needing to speak, not then, as the sun began to rise. Finally, Lauralen Flint rose to her feet and walked – Jack always remembered thinking that she had *glided* – to the edge of the lake.

The rising sun shone on her golden hair and made it glow. Jack was reminded of the time Corriwen had dived through the sky over the edge of the waterfall in Temair and he'd thought it was the most beautiful thing he had seen in his life. His mother was the most beautiful person he had ever seen.

The new light made her long gown seem gauzy and he could see damselflies beyond her as they silently skimmed the surface. For an instant, his vision seemed to waver then jump into startling focus.

She caught his look and an expression of aching sadness flitted across her face.

'What's wrong?' Jack broke the silence. 'There's something happening!'

She nodded. He stared at her. He could see the reeds on the far bank, still woven with mist, but he could see them faintly behind her, as if she was becoming wispy and insubstantial.

Lauralen Flint knelt in front of her son and took his hands in hers. Her skin felt like gossamer, as if it was hardly there at all. Then she spoke.

'Since our heartstones touched, there have been no secrets between us. All is revealed, your life, your father's and my own. The lives we have lived, the lives we now share. I have seen you grow, and I have lived your adventures, Journeyman of my heart. And now it is time.'

'I don't understand! What's wrong? You're ... you're *disappearing*!'

'You came for me, and together we prevailed. All of us. Your father and your fine friends and yourself. And the fight will go on. I know you are your father's son and I will always be with you, in the heartstone and in your heart.'

The sun sparkled on the water. It sparkled through her hair and through her eyes, as if she was filled with diamonds.

Jack was shaking his head, unable to speak, dreading what she might say.

'We were too long in the nether-world. The binding spell

I wove let me sleep in timeless safety where the beast could not reach me. It lured you down to its depths to bring the two hearts together and destroy them. It would have been the end of everything.

'But we prevailed and there will be harmony across the worlds, until the next evil arises. That will be your quest. Who knows where, or when, but the Journeyman must journey. The battle always waits.

'But we are no longer of the worlds of the living. Your father and I must travel on, and we must go now.'

'No!' Jack was aghast. His heart hammered against his ribs. A pain stabbed behind his eyes.

His father stepped out from the edge of the trees, as tall and strong as he had been when the statue on the red plain had shed its skin of stone. He held Hedda's magnificent sword in its scabbard. The great horn Jack had heard him blow when he was just a baby, was slung on his shoulder.

'Yes, Jack. Our time is gone and another world waits for us.'

'What world?' Jack was panicking. His heart beat wildly. Desperate anguish rose deep inside him. 'Don't go. I've just found you! You *can't* leave me now!'

Jonathan Flint strapped the sword to Jack's waist, weighed the horn on his son's neck and put both hands on his shoulders.

'Know that you are *always* with us, and will be with us again.'

Jonathan Flint was fading too. Jack could see the reflected dew through his father's face.

'But where are you going?'

'You know the place. From your books.'

'Tir-nan-Og!' Realisation struck him like a blow. 'The land of the young!'

Jack backed away, shaking his head.

On the far side of the lake, mist was beginning to roll out past the reeds and on to a grassy bank. It began to coil slowly into twin translucent pillars.

Between the pillars, a clear light shone.

'Walk with us,' his father said gently.

Jack shook his head. The tears were streaming down his cheeks. Words choked in his throat. The world seemed to spin.

His mother took his hand. Jonathan Flint put his arm around Jack's shoulders, but Jack could hardly feel its weight or his mother's touch. It was as if they were barely in this world at all. Together they led him round the water towards the shining gateway.

By now, his mother's face was almost translucent. But her eyes were the clearest blue, and regarded him with such profound love that his heart almost stopped.

Beyond the gateway a smooth road meandered to a little bridge over a stream. On the far side, rolling green fields stretched into the distance.

Across the fields, hundreds of people were walking towards the bridge. They looked like the old Celtic heroes and heroines that Jack had read about in the books he'd loved. Their faces were wreathed in smiles and they looked at peace.

They came over the fields to welcome the Lady Lauralen and Jonathan Cullian Flint.

Jack's mother kissed him on the forehead. It was like a breath of air. His father's hand was a featherweight on his shoulder and then it was gone.

Together they walked through the shining gateway, as their son watched them leave, and the sunlight of that other place made them whole again. They crossed the bridge and then they turned.

Jack's father nodded to him and waved his hand in silent farewell. His mother smiled.

Then the pillars turned back into mist and the gateway was gone.

Jack Flint was alone again.

THIRTY TWO

Jack picked up the great sword and slung the amberhorn bow on his back. Corriwen had sheathed her knives. Kerry's short-sword was gone, lost in the battle, but he still had his sling. Rionna walked with Megrin's staff and they approached the Homeward Gate of Uaine.

Kerry stopped some distance away. Between the carved stone pillars the air twisted and shimmered like a mirage. Beyond them stood the Cromwath Ringstones, and home.

But Kerry walked no further. Jack already knew.

For a while he had been utterly alone with his thoughts, feeling he would die from loss and grief. He thought the pain of it would never stop. His heart felt as if it had been wrenched out of him. Corriwen, Kerry and Rionna left him to grieve and he sat for a long time on a hill beyond the forest, lost in his own memories.

Now he was facing a second loss.

'I need a break, Jack,' Kerry had said, pleading for Jack's understanding. 'Honestly I do. Back there, back home I'm just the bottom of the heap. Just the raggedy-arsed Irish rascal. There's nothing for me there.'

Jack felt his stomach clench again. He couldn't take losing Kerry too.

'But after all we've been through,' he began. 'You can't just . . . walk away.'

'Who said I'm walking away? I never said that! I just want to sit down and not have to run or fight all the time. Jeez, Jack, we're not even fifteen. I want to enjoy myself for a bit.'

'Why not enjoy yourself back home?'

'Because all the other places we've been, I've been *somebody*. Even if it was somebody everybody wanted to kill. Over there, I'm *nobody*.

'I spoke to Rionna and I want to see her place. Look around, you know? Spend some time fishing. Maybe have a picnic.'

'But something else is going to happen,' Jack said. 'Some time. Who knows when? And I'll need you with me.'

'I didn't say I'm *quitting*,' Kerry assured him, eyes bright with tears that he brushed away angrily. 'No way, Jack. Just let me have some time to catch my breath where things aren't always trying to do me in. When you need me, I'll be right there.'

Kerry grabbed him in a tight hug and held him close.

'You and me and Corrie. All for one and each for everybody else. Same as always.'

'I'll come for you when the time's right,' Jack said.

'I'll be there.'

Jack Flint and Corriwen Redthorn stepped through the Homeward Gate.

There were thirteen standing stones and thirteen gateways between them. They stood together inside the ring.

'It's that one,' Jack pointed, preparing himself for this parting.

'I know where it is,' she replied, eyes bright. 'But that's not the way for me. Temair doesn't need me. You do.'

Corriwen strode forward and held him tight.

'Who knows when the next fight will be, the next quest. You need me at your back, and that's where I'll be.'

She smiled at him.

'Always.'

EPILOGUE

On a bright autumn day, a boy and a girl sat on the high wall that surrounded a very old woodland. The leaves were gold and the sun reflected silver from the estuary far down the hill.

High above, a jet drew a line of white across a clear sky and the girl stared at it, eyes wide and full of wonder as it arched above them.

Jack Flint had put the heartstone into its niche and watched the sun and moon flick eastwards across the sky as the key to worlds turned the clock back and back until he knew he had arrived at the beginning of his journeys.

As they sat on the wall, he took the great horn in his hands, raised it to his lips and sent out a deep booming note that echoed across the valleys on the peninsula where he had grown up.

'Might as well let the Major know we're coming,' he said. 'And with luck, he'll get the kettle on.'

They clambered down and began to cross the field to the big house.

'You'll love it here. A soft bed, good food. Great books. And the Major, well, he's special. He was my father's best friend.'

When he thought of his father, Jack's voice almost dried up, but he swallowed hard, then flashed Corrie a warm smile. It would take him a while to come to terms with it; and to let his heart heal. But he would get there.

Jack took Corriwen's arm, and together they walked in sunshine towards home.